Wake of Deception

Sasha DeVore

"… I would definitely recommend fans of dystopia to give this book a try." -Readers' Favorite

Wake of Deception

Library of Congress Cataloging-in-Publication Data

Wake of Deception/ Sasha DeVore- 1st ed.

Summary: Everything is under control. The Ancient Ones guide us now. As the final bomb was being dropped, they saved humanity from self-destruction. But Hanu and his friends are about to find out why they're really here, and it could cost them their lives.

ISBN 978-0-692-79377-0

[1. Dystopian- Fiction 2. Science Fiction- Fiction 3. Metaphysical- Fiction]

To my husband and son,
who've supported me every step of the way.
And to Lisa,
my first silent reading partner.

They Came

It wasn't like General Tsung needed to refer to his radar in order to figure out that he was flying over the right city. It was just a formality. He knew this route from the many missions he'd flown into the heart of America during these last nine years of war. It was beyond the risen Pacific, past the angry, earthquake- aggravated coastline of what used to be California and Nevada, and over desolate Utah: Colorado Springs. He could see the city just ahead now, still dazzling in some places where they hadn't yet bombed. It was here that he would drop the nuclear missile that would end the war.

And he wanted to look as charming and important as he could while he did it because this event, just like the rest of the bloody war, was being streamed live to the entire world. His children and grandchildren and great-grandchildren would bask in the glory of his contribution to their nation's victory, so he made sure to tell the terrified cameraman to only take photos of his good side.

So he adjusted the radar screen dramatically as he read the coordinates to his co-pilot.

"Confirming: 38.7372 degrees north, 104.8808 degrees west. We have approached our target. Prepare to release the missile."

The co-pilot, who had been sitting in silence for the latter half of the trip, quickly released the safety on the missile port and placed his hand over the lever that would drop the bomb. He looked to his General, waiting for him to give the nod.

Tsung's eyes studied the mountains. The President, along with most of his line of command, took refuge in the base here. He would wait until the right moment, until they were just close enough, to ensure that the mushroom cloud rose directly from the center of the mountain. At this point, aesthetics were really the only thing to consider.

When they were right on top of it, the General slowly dipped his chin.

"Releasing missile." And with a triumphant smile, the co-pilot pushed the lever forward.

For such a massive object, the bomb seemed to float effortlessly, peacefully, on the breeze. It seemed the rules of gravity didn't apply to it. The bomb tumbled toward its destination with a foreboding whine.

Several of the aircraft behind Tsung's captured the descent, sending footage to the few million people who had survived the war. They watched anxiously as the bomb approached detonation. Some people counted, just to see how long it would take before it went off. *One... two... three...* it cleared the stratosphere- *four...five...* heading straight for the peak now- *six...seven...* and it vanished.

Then there was the gasp heard 'round the world, as it went down in the textbooks. The ones who didn't make it to the television missed it, but if they had made it, they would've seen that a sparkling silver orb appeared and beamed the missile right out of the air. It happened in an instant. The orb, which looked like nothing more than a giant mass of mercury, pulsed toward the bomb and caught it with a red laser, then the missile disappeared.

People in their living rooms, and at crisis centers and pubs and shelters stared at each other in shock for a few brief moments. The excitement and fear were tangible. Within minutes of the miraculous appearance of the orb, something else began to broadcast over the TVs: a message. There was no image, only a wispy, but compassionate voice over grey static.

"Dear Young Ones, you have hated, bickered and warred for a very long time now. Can you not see more peaceful ways to disagree? Can you not imagine more industrious solutions to your problems? We have watched you interact with the world given to you, and you have brought us great joy… but you have also brought us great sorrow. You see, the current course of action will inescapably lead to your own annihilation."

"Soon, the entire planet will be uninhabitable. We have intervened on this occasion out of love and necessity, but the course of the future is up to you. We dare not intervene again without your permission, but if you would like, Young Ones, we extend a helping hand. So we are calling out to the people of Earth- we are asking you, do you wish for us to help you change your course of action? Do you wish for us to guide you toward a peaceful path of life in abundance? Think about this question. Search your heart deeply, and send up your answers. We will hear them."

Then there was a buzzing that grew louder and louder in the streets. The visitors inspired a hope that Earth hadn't felt in many years. People gathered in their schools, government buildings, neighborhoods and places of worship to talk. They debated the authenticity of the offer, and what it meant for them. Three days later, everyone had cast their votes, and the Ancient Ones landed.

They would hold a summit.

Wake of Deception

Chapter One

An Odd Morning

No one at the Flush necessarily wakes up in a good mood. As a matter of fact, the patients typically wake up in more of a no-mood. It's true, there wasn't a single child at the American Continental Mental Hospital that should have been experiencing any wide range of emotions at all. It gets too dangerous, given their unstable conditions and all.

That's actually how the hospital got its nickname- the Flush. The doctors, therapists and staff on this little patch of habitable land flush all of those erratic and dangerous emotions right out of you. That's the first step to having a truly peaceful world, according to the Ancient Ones.

So it was really quite unusual that Hanu awoke this particular Wednesday morning in what we would call a *very* good mood. He lay quietly in his metal cot, wide eyed and suspicious of the peculiar feeling. His heart was pounding. It was going to float up and out of his chest if he didn't breathe deeply enough. He felt like opening his mouth and bellowing at the top of his lungs. It felt *so* right.

Chapter One

But he couldn't. He knew that if he did, Ms. Jones would call the nurse and he would be getting booty-juice within the minute. That's what they called the injection you got when you started acting out of line. Nasty stuff. It burned going in and then you were knocked out for about twelve hours.

Mrs. Rand, the daytime nurse, always encouraged the patients to report these symptoms- elevated heart rate and swelling sensation in the chest; feelings of over excitability- so that they could receive the proper treatment for it. Once a month the psychiatrist would come and give his presentation with those little puppets about how dangerous it is to let these things get out of hand.

This feeling was pleasant, though. It made him feel nostalgic; as though he would soon remember some barely-out-of-reach memory that wanted to resurface. No, Hanu decided he would keep quiet about all of these feelings. He got out of bed and found his shoes in the dark. He moved about slowly so as not to trigger the motion activated camera that perched in the corner of the room. Everyone was monitored, and the children at the Flush were no different. But at least the Council had the decency to give them a little privacy as they slept or maybe sat in the corner and had a good cry.

Finding a comfortable place on the floor, Hanu sat with his legs crossed. He would wait until daybreak when Ms. Smith would finally come around and turn on his light to wake him. He breathed deeply and tried to calm his thoughts, hoping that the memory would return. He concentrated on it for quite some time.

An Odd Morning

And then it came. Or maybe he went. He was suddenly standing before a tall desk. He had to take a few steps back in order to see the creatures who sat behind it. There were seven of them. They were strange, with brown, wrinkled little faces and wispy whiskers protruding from underneath long beards. The room offered very little light, but he could see that they all wore maroon robes.

"You've been quite content to allow this to go on," one of the creatures said, leaning in to get a better look at Hanu. "You're dormant."

"I've been in no position to carry out this task. And besides…I don't want to become a martyr," Hanu told him solemnly.

"You've allowed fear to cloud your judgement. You will find your strength again," the old creature said with a comforting smile.

And then just as quickly as it had come, the memory began to fade. Or rather, the *dream* began to fade. Hanu realized that he had had a dream- the first one in years. He tried to hold on to every detail- the creatures' faces, the dark room, the words…

Mr. Carlisle, Hanu's therapist, once told him that dreams were windows to the subconscious. He said that since humanity's subconscious had been so badly distorted, they had to abandon dreaming all together because it would drive a person insane. Hanu thought maybe Mr. Carlisle was right, because the creatures he had dreamt up were quite ridiculous looking. And on top of that, he didn't know what a martyr was.

Chapter One

But at the same time he *wanted* to dream. He enjoyed the feeling that there was something more than his deranged existence.

Hanu could see the first light of the sun creeping into his room. It was close enough to daybreak, and he just couldn't wait any longer. He crept over to the doorway and knocked gently on the frame.

"Permission to do my morning hygiene?" he asked Ms. Jones.

Ms. Jones, the night staff, was sitting at the only table in the long hallway, finishing up the nights paperwork. She dimmed the screen on her computer and looked at Hanu for a few seconds, debating the question.

"Very well, I shall provide you a towel," she said curtly.

Hanu grabbed his hygiene box from underneath his desk and bounced down the hallway on the balls of his feet. He stopped at the door of the communal bathroom and waited for Ms. Jones to unlock it. Everything in this facility was locked- bathrooms, bookshelves, towel closets, and water fountains- so you spent a good portion of your day waiting for one thing or another to be opened for you.

Ms. Jones moved about, productively, preparing soap and towels for Hanu. All of the staff had that same air of productiveness. They hardly ever showed traces of distinct personality. Hanu and the other patients decided that maybe it was part of their training.

When she appeared at the bathroom door, she looked Hanu once over. He was only fourteen, but he was just as tall as she was. Her soft features didn't quite fit the baggy black staff jumper she was wearing. A princess' gown seemed more appropriate for her delicate frame.

"You awoke fourteen minutes early today. Yesterday it was seven minutes. Have you been feeling disturbed?" she asked.

Hanu hesitated. He would have liked to tell her that it was happiness he was feeling, but every time he mentioned such things to Mr. Carlisle he'd get a lecture about safe and unsafe feelings.

"I'm feeling…well, *not* disturbed," he said.

"I shall document that you completed your morning hygiene early again," she said, matter-of-factly. Then she straightened herself up as much as she could and looked him over once more before unlocking the door.

Confused, he entered the bathroom. He must've looked disturbed to her, he thought, because she was acting strange. He looked at himself in the wide mirror- first, from a side view, and then straight on. His hair fell around his face in tawny curls. Hanu's skin was usually pale, but today it was warm and radiant, sparkling with sweat.

He looked around even though he knew he was alone, then he looked back at himself and cracked a smile. He sometimes practiced smiling to see what it felt like, what it looked like on him. In all of the seven years Hanu lived at the hospital, his smile never conjured any particular feelings, and it definitely never looked quite like it was supposed to. His vacant eyes always cancelled out the upturned corners of his mouth in a very creepy way. But he practiced nonetheless, because of Titanya. She'd been living at the hospital for almost six weeks now, but she never stopped smiling. One day Hanu would return that congenial smile.

And today might be the day. Today's smile perfectly complimented this auspicious sensation he was feeling in his body. Hanu brushed his teeth and then treated himself to a long shower.

By the time the other patients had started entering the bathroom Hanu was finished. He put his towel in the community bin and headed back to his room. Jeremiah and Ester were sitting in front of the towel closet waiting for soap. No surprise seeing those two together. Jeremiah is the only one who can get Ester to talk- even if it's just with him in whispers- and Ester has a disturbing way of staring that only Jeremiah can tolerate. The two seemed a little livelier than usual as well, he thought to himself.

As Hanu passed Ester she acknowledged him with her usual penetrating stare. Hanu gave her his much practiced smile, which she answered with a knowing nod. He was taken aback. He stood in the hall for a moment, looking at Ester, expecting her to do something more, maybe even say something. She didn't. She had already moved on to staring at Les, who was coming to get soap, too.

Back in his room he folded his used rust-red jumpsuit and put it in his laundry basket, along with the rest of the week's accumulated items. Then, as he walked across the room to replace his hygiene box, Hanu noticed something unusual going on outside of his window.

He stood there, hygiene box still in hand, trying to make his brain recognize what he was seeing. Hanu must've sat at this window for hours a day, watching the comings and goings in the concrete courtyard below, but today something was happening that he had never seen before.

He could barely see the rising sun. It was being blocked out by white fog. Not the usual fog that the drones sprayed. And besides, the drones wouldn't be out this early anyway. They sprayed in the evening. This was a totally different fog. It was much thicker, and filled almost the whole sky.

Water was falling, too. Hanu could see it hitting the sidewalks and windows with a loud slapping sound. Where was it coming from? He stared out of the window, pondering the strangeness of the morning. The dream, Ester's nod, now falling water…this morning was turning out to be an odd one, he thought.

"Meds!" he yelled to no one. Realizing he was late for the morning medicine line, Hanu dropped his hygiene box and ran out of the room. Through the window at the end of the hall he could see that the sun, swathed in fog, was rising over the buildings now. He slowed to a brisk walk as he came down the corridor towards the social room and nurse's station.

To his relief Mrs. Rand was still passing out medicine. Hanu looked at the clock on the wall above the nurse's station window. It read 6:32. The line was still quite long for it to be so late. Hanu didn't complain, though. He situated himself at the back of the line, content with not having drawn any attention to himself.

In all the time Hanu's been here at the hospital he only missed the med line a couple of times before he figured out just how much he never wanted to do it again. He refused to take his meds for the first time when he was nine. It was an all-out temper tantrum. The medicine made his stomach hurt and he was already angry with Mr. Carlisle for telling him that his mother would stop visiting, so he spit all over the floor and yelled at the top of his lungs at anyone who walked by. That was the first time he went to containment for behavioral reprogramming. The second time was when he was twelve. Enough time had passed for him to forget just how bad containment was, but they quickly jogged his memory.

One patient, a long time ago, had been sent to containment so many times that they just went ahead and shipped him off to the Capital City for override. Hanu didn't know just how many times you had to mess up before that, and he didn't plan on finding out. That was a fate that he just didn't see in his own future. Which is why he had been so careful to show up on time for meds and make sure that nobody- not even the other patients- saw when he slipped his pills between his gums and lip.

From the back of the line, Hanu could see that the staff seemed a little restless today. At six in the morning they were usually bustling around- productively, of course- but today they were clustered in groups, whispering amongst themselves or rushing in and out of the nurse's station. Mr. Drews and Mrs. Pack, the weekend nurses, were also present.

The TV in the social room was displaying the morning news, as usual. The familiar holographic news anchors were projected into the room by a round lens in the ceiling. The man and woman always wore cordial expressions, and their wit livened up the place in the morning time. Hanu could barely hear what they were saying, but he didn't have to hear in order to know that today they were delivering bad news. At the bottom of the projection, revolving around the desk of the anchors was a bold red headline reading:

SABOTAGE ATTEMPTS CONTINUE. DISSENTERS MISS TARGET.

Hanu wondered if that was the reason the staff were acting so strange this morning. These attacks have been happening more frequently in the last few days. Two days ago Hanu heard Mr. Garret telling Ms. Santo that the Dissenters were trying to carry out some prophesy.

“It’s like a religious thing,” he said. “They think that humans need to overthrow the Ancients and create their own way of life, so they’re trying to kill enough people so that they can control the rest.”

“You'd think we'd learn from the past,” Ms. Santo sighed. “That’s the kind of thinking that led us to World War III. Leave humans alone and they blow the planet up… that’s exactly what we would’ve done if the Ancients hadn’t showed up when they did.”

“I know, right?” Mr. Garret agreed. “Look at us- almost a hundred years have passed and we’re still recovering from that war. And how can you go against the Ancient Ones anyway? That’s like going against a parent.”

“Well let’s hope they see reason and turn themselves in,” Ms. Santo went on. “If it were me, I would gladly ask for override. Why ruin life for everyone else just because *you're* miserable?”

Chapter One

Hanu sat by his bedroom door listening to their conversation that night. Apparently, the Dissenters had snuck some sort of device in the water treatment facility.

"What's going on?" A voice whispered in Hanu's ear, making him nearly jump out of his skin. He was so deep in thought that he didn't notice Akesh sneak in line behind him. Akesh was Hanu's closest friend. He was shorter than Hanu even though he was a full year older than him, and his black hair perpetually stuck out in all directions, as if it purposefully rebelled against his hairbrush.

"I don't know. Maybe they're…running behind today?" He replied more as a question than a statement. In all of the years Hanu lived at the hospital the staff never ran behind on anything. It was just unheard of.

Akesh rambled on, shifting his eyes toward the nurse's station. "Don't get me wrong, I'm glad the line's not moving. I totally stopped in the hallway for no reason at all, but it just felt right so I stayed there staring off into space. I'm so glad they didn't come looking for me 'cause this time it was an honest mistake."

Hanu agreed halfheartedly as he craned his neck to see what was going on at the front of the line, but Akesh didn't seem to mind.

"So what do you think about this new stuff they've been giving us?" he went on. "You know, the orange triangle? I like it, tastes a little like blood though… not sure what's up with that."

"Uh, I don't know, 'Kesh. It's okay, I guess," Hanu replied. He would've been able to give a more accurate review if he actually had been taking the medicine, but it didn't matter because Akesh had already moved on to fidgeting with the fake tree that was potted in the corner behind them.

Akesh enjoyed taking his medicine and often got too excited in the med line, so holding a full length conversation was near impossible. Sometimes when they got up to the window he'd ask for extra medicine for made up aches or anxiety- a request which the nurse was always happy to be obliged. The medicine doesn't seem to have an effect on Akesh, therapeutic or otherwise, but he does enjoy comparing tastes and textures of the different drugs.

Honestly the new medicine was a mystery that Hanu had actually spent a lot of time considering. Mrs. Rand said it was to concentrate the treatment for his schizophrenia, but everyone at the hospital was required to take it. And moreover, she wasn't going to inform him that he was prescribed a new drug. He just so happened to notice the orange mixed in with his usual assortment that morning. It was when they first tried to slip him that little pill, about two weeks ago, that Hanu decided he was finished with his medications.

As the two friends made their way to the front of the line, Hanu prepared for his med-cheeking technique. It was imperative that he not get caught, so he had to look and act as calm and relaxed as he could. He would be friendly, but not too friendly- and he wouldn't doddle. Maybe today he would complement Ms. Rand's scrubs again. Last time she blushed, looking down at her ensemble just long enough for him to tuck the six multicolored capsules between his lip and gums with his tongue.

Chapter One

But he never got a chance to follow through with his plan. Just as he was stepping up to the window at the nurses station the TV jumped to full volume. Hanu turned and saw the staff running into the social room where the other patients had taken their seats and continued to stare as if nothing at all were unusual. The two anchors were now replaced by a lone reporter who was standing in front of a mountainous landscape.

“Program, mute,” one of the staff commanded. But his voice continued to blare.

“…possible target was the Regional Food Production Facility located to the Southeast of these mountains. We can assume that their intent was to halt the distribution of food to the region, which would affect virtually everyone on the continent, but you can see here, the missiles that were fired around two A.M. landed here in the mountains, causing very little damage,” he said as he walked along the foothills of the mountain. In several places behind him there were smoldering columns. Then the usual anchors returned, and the woman was changing the subject.

“On a brighter note, Super Bowl celebrations will still be held as scheduled. Officials say that the Bowl will-”

But the staff must’ve gotten the program to mute because Hanu could no longer hear their voices. He couldn’t hear anything, actually. Hanu looked around, confused. Then his eyes jerked around without his permission, their muscles firing off rapidly. Trying to keep himself oriented, he attempted to focus on the people in the room, but he was no longer able to make sense of what he was seeing. Everyone was blurry, like they were shrouded in heat waves. Hanu looked at Akesh, who was saying something to him, but he couldn't get his eyes to adjust.

Hanu's body felt weak. He tried to grasp the rail but found that he couldn't move his arms. And he couldn't open his mouth to call for help, either, because his jaws were locked. His eyes finally stopped twitching, but he could only look forward at Akesh. Then he was only able to look at the ceiling as staff members closed in around him.

Hanu closed his eyes.

Chapter Two

The Hospital Wing

Hanu awoke with a ringing in his ears. He kept his eyes closed and listened, concentrating on the sensation. It wasn't really a ringing. No, it wasn't a sound he was hearing at all. He was feeling it, rather. His ears were warm and full- as if the canals were slowly expanding, filling up with noiseless sounds. For several minutes he lay there motionless, willing his ears to hear it.

Then Hanu actually did hear something. A scraping noise. Metal against metal. It was very close to his face, actually. Hanu opened his eyes to look for the source of the sound, and was surprised to find Akesh standing over a small tray next to his bed. He was snooping through the various instruments and medical supplies on it.

"They didn't give you anything good, then, huh?" he said, noticing that Hanu was awake now. Hanu sat up. They were in the hospital wing.

"What are you doing here, 'Kesh?" he asked.

"I'm visiting, of course. Mr. Walsh is escorting me. He's in the bathroom right now, though," Akesh said, putting on a pair of plastic gloves.

The Hospital Wing

Hanu looked around. He hardly ever had reason to visit the hospital wing. It was rather like his bedroom, actually. But that wasn't surprising, as there wasn't much variation from wing to wing. Just like his living quarters, the hospital room had bare white walls and a large plaque of the rules and protocols. Beyond the metal tray next to his bed there was a desk with several instruments, and above it was a small square window with thick glass. It displayed a different courtyard than the one Hanu's bedroom window faced. Hanu looked up into the sky. The water was no longer falling.

"How long have I been here?" he asked. An IV was in his arm and he could feel a tube running from his nose into his throat.

"All day. It's seven o' clock by now," Akesh said, looking anxious. "Hanu are you feeling okay? You passed out and…"

"I feel alright now. Earlier I don't know what happened. My body just kind of... locked up."

"Hanu, I really hope you're okay. I just feel…" and his voice trailed off. Sometimes Akesh got really sentimental and then things got weird. Hanu knew it was because he was a really sensitive person, and he liked that about him. They learned to just skirt around that kind of stuff, though, to keep some semblance of normalcy in their lives.

"Enough about me, what about you?" Hanu asked brightly.

"Well, today they told me that I was invited into the District!" he said excitedly. Hanu was taken aback. Akesh doubled over, laughing at the terror on his face. "No, they're taking a group of us into the District as special guests to watch the Bowl. It's in Asia this year, so they're setting up a huge party. It's the

South American Suns against the Pan Asia Dragons. We're going to be in the parade and everything!"

"Oh that sounds way more awesome than override," Hanu exhaled, relieved.

"Yeah, I know. My therapist said they invited us this year to show support for the Flush. Afterward they'll be doing some research to help our treatment and stuff. I think it's some publicity stunt, but hey, I'm going to a Bowl party!" he said, dancing around the room now.

"Hey, you quiet down!" said Mr. Walsh, rushing into the room and scaring the boys half to death. "You're disturbing the whole floor!"

Then the nurse came in, looking back and forth from Hanu, now sitting up in the bed, to Akesh, arms still raised in a celebratory dance.

"Well it looks like you've had your visit, dears. Out!" she said, rushing them out of the room. Once they had cleared the room she turned to Hanu.

"Dear, you're supposed to be resting. Doctor's orders," she said as she took his vitals. Then she adjusted the drip in the IV. "I'm going to give you a little dose of medicine to help you get back to sleep. Rest up, now."

"But I've been asleep for like twelve hours," he argued. It was too late, though. He was already drowsing.

Hours later Hanu was swimming in a state of half sleep. His body just refused to slumber any longer, but the medicine was still in effect. Hanu blinked a few times, trying to shake the feeling. The sun was coming up. He had slept for a whole day.

Hanu could hear voices now, and was afraid. Not that it was unusual for him to hear voices, he heard them all the time. But he was afraid it was the nurse coming to give him more sleeping medicine. He closed his eyes again and pretended to still be asleep.

Then he recognized the voices. They were real, and thankfully not the nurse's. They belonged to people he actually knew. Hanu sat up and tried to hear what they were saying.

The door was cracked just slightly. He could hear Ms. Jones and Mr. Carlisle, talking with a third person whose voice was unfamiliar.

"In your prognosis notes you never mentioned he was waking up by himself," Mr. Carlisle said to Ms. Jones.

"I guess I wasn't as explicit as I should have been. However, I did mention that he was doing his morning hygiene earlier than usual," she said defensively.

"That's neither here nor there," the third person began. He spoke slowly as if he were bored or uninterested. "What is important is that we were able to minimize this incident. We're lucky this happened yesterday, of all days. With current arrangements, it was easy to make accommodations."

Hanu realized they must've figured out he wasn't taking his medicine. Of *course*, he thought. Everyone takes sleeping pills at night, so it would be obvious if he was waking up on his own all of a sudden. Hanu began to feel uneasy about the accommodations this man was talking about.

Ms. Jones continued. "That is all very well, but how will I be reprimanded?" she asked in anxious tones.

Hanu wondered what kind of punishment staff got for incompetence. He imagined Ms. Jones being taken in for behavioral reprogramming.

"I wouldn't worry about it too much," said Mr. Carlisle. "The nurses will get more flack about it than anyone else on the team."

"Are you two sure there is nothing more you would like to record? The unfamiliar man asked. After a few moments of silence they must've shaken their heads. The man continued.

"Alright, Ms. Jones you may go and get some sleep. Thank you for your cooperation."

"Thank you, goodbye," she said, and Hanu heard her footsteps grow feint down the hall.

"Can I ask you a question, Mr. Wolfe?" said Mr. Carlisle.

"Of course," he replied.

Mr. Carlisle lowered his voice, speaking more urgently now. "You transport patients and information into the District all the time. Have you heard about the new drugs they're mandating? First the RiboBan and now this inhalant they started giving yesterday. What're they for, and why are they keeping the therapists in the dark about it?"

"I'm a simple transport agent-," Mr. Wolfe began in his drawling voice, but Mr. Carlisle cut him off.

"Look, if it's a matter of security that you can't tell me, I'll just have to get over it. But I know you can attend the briefings with the Council and they just had one a few weeks ago. I know you know what's going on," he said.

"I did attend that briefing last month," Mr. Wolfe admitted. "Honestly, Mr. Carlisle, we are just in a…*unique* situation. The Council has reason to believe that the Dissenters are trying to strengthen their numbers. They may be trying to prey on the weak and unbalanced members of society," Mr. Wolfe said.

"You think they want to recruit mental health patients?" Mr. Carlisle asked, almost laughing.

"It's not a matter of what I think," said Mr. Wolfe. "It's a matter of keeping these patients safe, for the good of society. If you've noticed, in the last few days they've tightened security around the habitable zone here as well."

There was a long silence. Hanu strained his ears to hear more, and was startled when the door suddenly swung open. Mr. Carlisle stood in the hallway with his back turned to Hanu.

"I'm sure this goes without saying, Mr. Carlisle, but don't repeat any of this to any of the patients or residential staff," Mr. Wolfe warned in a lowered voice.

Hanu took this opportunity to relax his body and close his eyes, feigning sleep. He heard Mr. Carlisle's footsteps cross the room to the empty chair. For several minutes Hanu kept his body still, afraid of being discovered. This proved to be quite difficult because trying to keep his breathing slow and even made his lungs protest at the lack of oxygen.

Chapter Two

Deciding he couldn't keep up the façade for much longer, Hanu rolled on his side and slowly opened his eyes. Mr. Carlisle was sitting in the chair, his dark beady eyes were fixed on his computer. After typing up his notes, Mr. Carlisle minimized the screen and placed the small device into his briefcase. As he leaned back and tousled his dark brown hair, he noticed Hanu watching him.

"You had a seizure," Mr. Carlisle said.

"Oh." Hanu didn't know how else to respond.

"How are you feeling? You were out for almost a whole day," he said, looking at his watch.

"I'm feeling fine. Akesh came to visit me yesterday. Told me he'd be in the parade next week." Hanu sat up in the bed and noticed he had a red blemish on the inside of his left wrist.

"What's this?" he asked, running his fingers over it. It felt warm.

"Hanu when they ran your blood test the doctors found that you had very small traces, if any of your medications at all." Mr. Carlisle's face was inscrutable. "When we renewed your treatment goals you said you wanted to shut out the voices so that you could go back home. You know that taking your medicine on schedule will help you to achieve that goal, Hanu."

"For seven years I've tried. *Seven.* I've taken my meds, I've cooperated with staff, and I've been honest during our sessions," Hanu said through gritted teeth. "After seven years you'd think I'd be cured!" he continued, raising his voice now.

"You've made significant progress in that time, Hanu," Mr. Carlisle began calmly.

"*Progress, Progress*," Hanu interjected, mocking Mr. Carlisle. Hot poisonous flames welled up inside Hanu's gut, and were forcing their way out of his mouth. "That's all anyone in this place ever talks about. As long as there's progress you keep your job, right? You don't care about curing us, you just keep pumping us with drugs. Oh, guess what? My kidneys are failing because of my medicine. That's alright, I've got more medicine to fix that! How can people be born so messed up when the Ancients came back and fixed all of our problems?"

Hanu didn't know why he was being so rude. He actually liked and respected Mr. Carlisle. But he couldn't help it; he couldn't keep the words that had been churning deep within him from finally spilling out. Hanu got out of the bed and started pacing the room. The flames pulsed through his entire body now, threatening to burn him alive if he sat still any longer.

"Makes no sense to me," he continued, speaking more to himself than Mr. Carlisle. "I do everything they ask… all this technology…gifts from the *Ancient Ones*," Hanu said, mocking reverence when he said 'Ancient Ones'.

Mr. Carlisle sat patiently in his chair, allowing Hanu to vent. "It's not even like I'm dangerous!" he barked. "What does it even matter that I can see things no one else can? What if you're the messed up ones? You can't even see things that are right in front of you!" he said, pointing to a spot right in front of Mr. Carlisle's face. He knew the man couldn't see the dark spiraling anomaly, but he was convinced that it was a fault of Mr. Carlisle's, and not his own.

Chapter Two

Hanu raised his pointed finger up to his temple- thumb sticking straight up- and pretended to shoot himself in the head, slumping dramatically onto the bed. Of course, Hanu didn't know what this actually meant, but he'd seen some of the more defiant patients do this gesture much to the dismay of their therapists.

"I guess I'm going to containment now," he said.

Mr. Carlisle looked at Hanu dejectedly. "No, you won't be going for behavioral reprogramming this time, Hanu."

Hanu sat straight up in the hospital bed, looking at his therapist.

"They've already implanted your trade interface," Mr. Carlisle said, indicating the mark on Hanu's wrist. "You'll need it to get into the District of Operations. You'll have to join the patients that were requested by the Council."

Chapter Three

Traveling Misfits

Hanu spent the next hour in silent acquiescence. He allowed himself to be escorted to the living unit by Mr. Carlisle. There, he packed his few true belongings- his sneakers, a toothbrush, a framed photo of his mom holding him and his little sister, and a large collection of socks. Then he was allowed one last shower and a clean jumper.

After Hanu said goodbye to the staff and some of the more interested patients, his therapist led him through the social room and unlocked the door that led to the courtyard.

Hanu stood in the doorway and looked back one final time, regretting not having said a proper goodbye to Akesh. If he'd known that yesterday would be the last time seeing him, he would've said much more. Hanu would've told him that he didn't think anything was wrong with him, that he was fine just the way he was. And he would've made sure Akesh knew that he was Hanu's best friend. He maybe would've hugged him, even. But according to Mr. Garrett, he was with his therapist for the morning. Well, maybe Hanu would get to see him in the District of Operations after the Bowl- that is, if Hanu was still alive.

Chapter Three

He equally regretted not being able to return a smile to Titanya. However, he did get a chance to say goodbye to her. Before packing all of his things he went into the social room to collect the black duffle bag he brought with him all those years ago. While Mr. Garrett was unlocking the storage closet to retrieve it, he walked over to speak to her. She was sitting on the ugly moquette bench that nobody ever chose if other seats were available. Hanu put his hand on her shoulder and said, 'smile always'.

She always exuded calmness, which lately inspired Hanu, but today he just couldn't be consoled enough to smile with her. Titanya scrunched up her face and chuckled, 'sure thing, Hanu'. Then he walked off rather awkwardly, feeling her eyes on his back. He wasn't quite sure why he said that, and now thinking back on it he probably just ensured her a few more prescriptions with that bit of advice. He wondered how many more weeks it would take before that smile faded for good.

Hanu finally turned around and walked through the door, kicking himself. He often fantasized about the day he would be walking through this courtyard to the discharge office- the day he would go home to his mother and baby sister. *Well, she's not a baby anymore*, he told himself. His sister, Kait, would be eight by now. It was somewhere around her first birthday that his teacher and the principals at his school called his mother in for a meeting. He remembered because he had to wait in the hallway with Kait that day. She was learning to walk at that point, and kept wailing and kicking to get out of his lap. But when he let her down she would just bumble into people and furniture, so he'd have to pick her up again. It was on that day they tried to convince his mom to take him in for testing because he always talked about events and voices nobody else seemed to notice. Hanu wondered how much Kait had changed in the last seven years.

He had to wait to find out, because now he had to go to the District of Operations. This mysterious walled sector deep within the Capital City was reserved for politicking among the Council and the Ancient Ones. The general public could only speculate on the types of activities that actually went on in the superstructure, but they were convinced it was nothing short of magic. For what reason they'd be requesting a group of mental health patients, Hanu was unsure. But maybe if he cooperated he'd be in a better position to return home.

Hanu tried not to allow himself to entertain the possibility that he was going in for override. *Then again, I'd been cheeking my meds for quite some time*, he reminded himself. That was grounds for severe punishment in and of itself. But still, the Council never just requests a group to override. Patients had to be recommended by their treatment team and then parents had to be notified. It was a whole process. Hanu went back and forth in his mind, trying to convince himself that he definitely wasn't going to die.

Approaching the discharge office at the far end of the courtyard, Hanu could see several other patients in the lobby. To his surprise Ester was there, along with two other girls from his unit. One of the girls, whose red hair served as a warning sign, was called Sadie. She sometimes broke out in unexpected fits of anger, so Hanu learned to never stand in her vicinity for too long at one time. He does respect her from a distance though, as she is one fun character. She also suffers from paranoia, but unlike Hanu, she's not afraid to call anyone out when she thinks they're lying.

Hanu didn't remember the other girl's name, but he often saw her trying to convince the staff that she was cured and that her therapist recommended her immediate discharge. This girl kept her blonde hair in a very short cut because she often complained that things were crawling in it.

There was also a younger girl with braids and twin boys from the unit that housed the younger patients. Hanu moved from that unit when he turned twelve. The twins sat erect in their seats, arms crossed and wearing identical scowls on their faces. Three nervous looking staff members stood directly behind them. They were alert enough to respond to any behaviors, but they were also aloof enough to not aggravate them either.

Mr. Carlisle checked Hanu in at the front desk and then said his goodbyes, closing the door with a loud click. Standing in the doorway, Hanu surveyed the group.

"Let's not waste a minute more. We're already behind schedule," a feathered woman shrilled as she crossed the room to collect Hanu's bag.

She was wearing a turquoise and yellow dress with an excessive amount of frills and high heeled boots so tall that only her toes touched the floor. Her jet black hair was pulled into a tight bun behind her head and she wore several layers of white eyeliner, making her eyes look orb like. Like many of the holographic actresses, she wore black blush on her cheeks, making her pale face appear skinnier than it already was. Hanu didn't know this woman's name, but he often saw her walking here and there through the courtyard, always looking equally as eccentric. Seeing her this close was downright alarming, though.

She grabbed Hanu's bag from his hands and turned to walk away, revealing the stupidest bow Hanu had ever seen pinned right between her shoulder blades. She shoved the bag into one of the staff member's hands.

"Mr. Ervin, please load that with the rest of the luggage, will you babe?" she said.

"Of course, Annabelle," Mr. Ervin said as he turned on his heels. Annabelle rounded on the desk and entered a code into the speaker system.

"Mr. Wolfe, would you guys come up? We're ready to sign over the patients," she chimed into the receiver.

"On our way," said the now familiar monotonic voice of Mr. Wolfe.

Without saying anything further she hung up and grabbed a metallic wand from somewhere behind the desk.

"Alright, children let's get you out of here," she said excitedly, turning to the group. "Everyone please stand up and form a line. As soon as the transport team gets here I will scan your trades and you can be on your way!"

Just as the group shuffled into a discernable line, three robed men and a scout arrived through a door behind the desk. Hanu was beginning to feel the authenticity of his situation. To have a scout as part of their escort was basically the same as having an Ancient One present. These innocent looking agents, dressed in boyish uniforms, were created for nothing more than intensive surveillance. They were peacekeepers, but Hanu always felt certain that they were used for other, maybe more sinister, things as well.

“Ladies first,” Mr. Wolfe said, inviting the receptionist to scan herself first. He seemed quite aloof, with his salt and pepper beard, offering no further gestures of cordiality.

Anabelle waived the metal wand over her own wrist, pulling up her profile on a holographic screen. Next Mr. Wolfe scanned himself. This changing of hands took place in a matter of seconds, after which Mr. Wolfe walked over to the door behind the desk and held it open.

She scanned one of the twins. His holographic profile only revealed the boys picture with his name and age underneath: Tui Feng, 9. Annabelle motioned for Tui to go through the door that Mr. Wolfe was holding. Next, his brother, who was named La. Then Sadie and the other girl from his unit, who happened to be named Vanessa. Hanu was thoroughly curious by the time it was his turn.

He remembered back to a time before the hospital when he accompanied his mother to the Food Distribution Center. They had waved a wand just like this over her wrist, but her profile looked a lot more impressive. Under her picture it read: Kara Manel, 39, Genetics Advisory Committee. It also showed her address, bank account balance, social network map, and food and water credits. Hanu couldn’t wait to get a trade of his own, but he would have to wait until he was sixteen. Then, he would be a grown up.

Annabelle finally waved the wand over Hanu’s wrist. A screen appeared, revealing his picture, along with his name and age, but the feeling of being a grown-up was somehow diminished. Hanu shuffled through the door into a very narrow corridor, rejoining the group. At the other end, there was another door. They quietly waited for everyone else to be scanned, trying not to breathe on each other or lock eyes for too long. Only after Ester and the girl with the braids entered the passageway did Mr. Wolfe and the other staff follow. He squeezed his way to the other door and addressed the group.

"I want you all to look around. This is the group that has been invited into the District of Operations. I will introduce your escorts. In the back- Mr. Ervin, Mr. Trattonere, and Ms. Felix- your residential staff." The three staff, distinguishable by their black jumpers, gave a nod at their introduction. "These gentlemen are my assistants-Mr. Assieger and Mr. Helm. As you can see, a scout will be traveling with us today, to ensure our safe arrival."

Hanu was wondering if the scout was ensuring that the escorts were safe from the patients, or that the patients were safe from the Dissenters.

"Without further delay, we will begin our journey, being as we are running behind. Once I open this door, we will quickly board and be on our way," he concluded. Then he unlocked the door and led them into a rather large indoor port.

This was the same port through which Hanu arrived years earlier. The loading dock gave way to a single elevated rail and a strip of metal street that ran parallel to it. This magnetized railing was the only track in the port, suited for one train- the one that took you from the Flush to the Capital City. There were only five cities on the continent, and they weren't meant to be traveled among so freely.

Chapter Three

These small cities were on the fringe of the Capital, and they were reserved for water sourcing, food production, University, international and space travel, and of course, mental health. And they only housed the production workers and scouts that were assigned to those duties. There was never really any traffic here, except the patients who were brought in and discharged or the staff who would travel to the Capitol on their days off. It was more efficient this way, according to the Ancient Ones.

The guideway of this port was vacant, though. Instead of the train, there was a large sleek vehicle pulled right beside the dock. It was a Convoy. Unlike the train, it didn't require a track. He'd seen these before, rarely, as well as other smaller vehicles called Nomads. When he was out and about with his mother, sometimes he'd see them on the narrow streets in the city. They were always either going to or from the District- official business, his mom would say. He'd definitely never been in one before.

"Why aren't we taking the Maglev?" Hanu asked the man named Mr. Assieger.

"As a matter of convenience," the man said, gruffly.

"Convenience, yes," added the scout. "For the sake of timelier travel, we'll be taking a Convoy. The train makes two stops- one just inside the habitable zone, and another at the inner rung of the city- before turning around. With the Convoy we'll travel directly into the District of Operations without interruption. The Convoy uses the same magnetic levitation as the train, so we'll still be traveling at optimal speed. For these advantages, transports directly into the District of Operations are always done by Convoy."

"Uh, thanks," Hanu said, uncertainly. He didn't expect the scout to be so thorough.

One by one, the passengers took their seats, according to Mr. Wolfe's seating chart. Hanu sat between Ester and the staff member called Mr. Trattonere. It was comforting, being next to her. Though they never technically had a conversation, he knew her better than anyone else in the Convoy. True, that little staring thing was unsettling, but Hanu was comforted by it now. He felt as though Ester would be watching his back.

The interior of the vehicle was of a soft, black material, and it was deceivingly spacious. The ceiling was tall enough for the passengers to stand up and move about freely. Seats were placed around various tables, and there was a small bar that was decorated with various muffins and wrapped candies. If Hanu wasn't so utterly terrified of what the end of this journey might entail, he would've enjoyed the comfort. He might've even asked to have something to eat from the bar. He hadn't had real sugar in years.

After everyone was seated, Mr. Helm took his place at the control panel. He stuck a small rectangular key into a port and typed up a few notes on the computer. Then he programmed a course for District of Operations.

"We should be arriving in two hours," he announced.

Mr. Wolfe closed the doors and took his seat. The children inspected the inside of the vehicle, impressed. Then Hanu looked up and was surprised. He didn't even realized they had taken off until the scenery in the windows changed.

Chapter Four

Escaping Reality

Everyone sat silently, witnessing the desolation of the land through which they traveled. As far as the eye could see in any direction was dead dirt, devastated by the nuclear blasts from the final war almost a hundred years ago. They passed by a warped, green, glasslike epicenter where a bomb exploded. Orange scars spiraled outward from it like a giant whirlpool sculpted into the ground. It was beautifully eerie.

Hanu wondered what might have been there before. Maybe it was a beautiful city, or perhaps a small forest or lake. In school last year, they learned about different topographies that existed before the war. His teacher told the class that this land was one of the wealthiest and most beautiful countries in the world. Now, the metal road and the guideway were the only signs of civilization. Hanu was certain there wouldn't be any Dissenters out in this wasteland.

"So I was in the hospital," Hanu said, breaking the silence. "I don't really know why we're going into the District of Operations. Can someone fill me in?"

Sadie, who was also looking out of the window turned around in her seat. "That's a good question, Hanu. I think we all deserve a few more details," she said, eyeing the scout.

The rest of the passengers looked to Mr. Wolfe, both children and adults alike. Nobody really seemed one hundred percent sure, and Mr. Wolfe was clearly the leader in this operation.

"It's not often at all that the Council requests an audience with the general public, so it's a great honor that they have invited you into the district," Mr. Wolfe assured them. "Most of you have never seen a member of the Council in person, let alone the inside of those great walls. The truth of the matter is, they are concerned about the effectiveness of the treatment you are receiving at the hospital. The council will be presenting this situation to the Ancients in order to find some solutions, but they will need to do some research first. That is why they have requested an audience with you."

Then the little girl with the braids spoke up in a mousy voice. "That's a great honor and all, but what kind of research are they going to do? Nothing....*painful*, right?" She was so small that Hanu had forgotten she was there.

"They'll be working with the Ancients, as they always do in tough situations, Zazi," Ms. Felix said. "Surely whatever they must do, they have the technology and wisdom to be fair and gentle. And besides, the Ancients chose them to be our leaders for a reason. They will be kind."

"That ain't cuttin' it for me," Sadie interjected. "Look at us, we're the worst ones in the hospital. I think they wanna get rid of us, and it's just easier to do us in all in one go. I know they're taking me in for override. I'm already at the age limit, and as you can tell, I'm not changing for nobody."

Chapter Four

"Speak for yourself, Sadie, I'm perfectly fine," Vanessa said. And it would've been halfway convincing had she not broken out into hysterical laughter just then. Mr. Ervin and Ms. Felix looked at each other with raised eyebrows. Ester continued looking out of the window, seemingly lost in her own thoughts. Her black bangs rested on her forehead, covering up her brows and most of her eyes, so Hanu couldn't really see her expression, if she had one.

"Let's ask the scout. Scouts can't lie," suggested one of the twins.

"You're so stupid, La. Of course they can lie. They work for the Ancients and the Ancient Ones are liars. They just say that in the stupid commercials to make you trust them," said Tui.

Hanu had seen the same commercial. The one where the scouts were walking around amongst the citizens, as they usually do. One was helping a child cross the street to get to the public park, another was holding the door for a woman walking into the Food Distribution Center and yet another was stopping a man in an apartment building and asking to scan his trade. The voiceover at the end of the commercial always reminds the viewers, 'the scouts are here to serve and protect us. Always honest, always there.'

"Okay that's enough boys," Mr. Ervin said, looking at the scout nervously.

The scout sat, quietly watching and unaffected by the speculation. His handsome face-identical to the rest of the artificial humans- seemed incapable of expressing any emotion, or it was probably more precise to say that he was incapable of *feeling* any emotion. His countenance was of boyish innocence, as usual.

In the real world, speaking against the Ancient Ones was kind of taboo. It wasn't a law or anything, but you could guarantee that any given person off the street would feel a sense of unease and foreboding if someone just came out and started speaking ill of them. And to do it in front of a scout was basically like doing it right to their faces.

Even Sadie knew that they had overstepped their boundaries, especially since they were probably on their way to meet one right now. Everyone went back to looking out of the windows.

For several minutes they sat, looking at the scarred land again. Every once in a while Vanessa would laugh or stand up and sit back down, and Zazi laid her head in Ms. Felix's lap. Mr. Ervin was about to unwrap a muffin when La yelled out.

"Look, creatures!" he exclaimed.

"Yeah, I see them, too," said Vanessa, who had stopped putting on airs miles ago. "There's one in the corner, and some in my hair. Hell, that guy ain't even human!" she said, jamming her thumb in the general direction toward the front of the vehicle. She chuckled to herself.

"No, you idiot. Real creatures," said La, pointing out of his window. Hanu hadn't noticed that the scenery had changed to lush jungle. They were moving very fast, but there was no mistaking it- they were passing by large animals.

Chapter Four

"Those are called elephants. There are several types of animals that inhabit this holographic jungle," the scout explained. "The Council thought it would be a nice touch to cast it around the habitable zone and fill it with the animal life that we shared the planet with not so long ago. It gives us a glimpse of the planets former beauty, and inspires a diverse future to work toward."

"What do you mean, inspires a diverse future?" Tui said, bitterly. "These animals are dead. Stupid humans killed them!"

"Yes, but with genetic engineering, the Ancients have been working toward recreating these animals. In the near future, they will be releasing real animals into the wild," explained the scout.

"What wild?" Sadie began. Hanu knew where this was going, so he quickly changed the subject.

"So we're here already, huh? We've reached the habitable zone?" he asked. He was actually growing quite nervous. They may possibly be meeting with the Ancient Ones, who more than likely heard the group blaspheming against them, so that they could do some vaguely explained research.

He wondered what Ester was thinking. She sat so calmly, confidently. She hadn't spoken a word since they left. *And probably never will, since Jeremiah's not here*, he thought, chuckling to himself.

The holographic jungle gave way to very real apartment buildings in the Residential District. They all looked exactly the same- cinder block boxes, six floors high and three units across. These buildings surrounded the city, just as the jungle had, in concentric circles. Hanu thought about his home somewhere among those apartment buildings.

It was hard to tell which one was his, being as they all looked the same. And besides, he hadn't been home for seven years, so he really didn't even remember which general direction to look in. But he did remember the floors in his apartment. When he was younger, he would always roll around on the smooth wood. His mother hated it because she would sometimes walk into a room just to trip over him. Sometimes he targeted her feet on purpose, just for fun.

And he remembered the moss shower mat that he begged his mom to buy for his bathroom. When Kait learned to crawl he had to keep his bathroom locked because she would go in there and try to eat the moss.

Hanu wondered if his mom had gotten new couches by now. The red ones they had were so tattered from years of wear and tear. One time Hanu pretended to be an Ancient One riding around in a space ship. He'd always wanted to take a ride in one, but apparently you could only do that under special circumstances, so the best he could do was imagine what it was like. Well one day he put a sheet over one of the couches, but the sheet kept smothering him and he couldn't see where he was steering the ship, so he stabbed a hole in the center of the couch and inserted the broom as a support column. It worked perfectly, but his mother wasn't too impressed when she found out about it.

The Convoy slowed as they entered one of the narrow streets of the Capital City. Slowly, they wound their way toward the center, passing parks, schools, surveillance towers…

Chapter Four

Hanu had been away for so long he forgot what life was like in the city. The people looked so strange to him now. Sometimes people wore casual clothing, like tee shirts and slacks, but at certain times of year they tend to get more festive. He watched them walk along the wide sidewalks through the windows of the Convoy like a silent movie. Each person seemed to be on a mission to out dress the last. They passed one woman wearing a golden pantsuit with a furry neckline and extremely pointy shoulders, and another wearing a spotted hat so tall that she had to stoop to get into the apartment lobby. Zazi pointed out a man wearing grey thigh high boots, spanks and body glitter.

This, in and of itself, wasn't all that strange. The Council often encourages the public to express themselves, and Hanu was used to animal themes as fashion inspiration by now. It was when they passed each other that Hanu noticed the strange part. It made him feel deeply uneasy, though he didn't know why. They weren't looking at each other. They weren't even acknowledging each other's existence. One man became extremely interested in his fingernails just as he passed another to get into a supply store. Then a very ornate woman went out of her way to ignore an elderly man passing by on the sidewalk, and he seemed quite relieved by it. Hanu wondered if it had always been like this here. Had he ignored people as he walked by? Hanu tried to think back on what it was like to walk down the street with his mother. He couldn't remember. But he did know one thing, when he got back home he would say hi to everyone who crossed his path, stranger or not.

As they passed into the Entertainment District Hanu saw friendlier people. Outside of a bar was a man sitting amongst a group of women in bathing suits. They sat with their feet in a wading pool, laughing and joking around.

"Looks like someone's having a good time," Hanu said aloud.

"More holograms. They liven up the place," Mr. Ervin explained. He must've had a lot of experience in the Entertainment District, Hanu mused. Laughing to himself, he imagined skinny Mr. Ervin with swim trunks on and surrounded by girls.

The children, who had never had any reason to venture this far into the city, were quite impressed by the grandeur of the place. Beaches, body builders and artful statues abutted otherwise ordinary cinder buildings and neon signs were scattered throughout the streets. Though it was daytime, they could almost imagine how the street would come to life with color after nightfall. Vanessa squealed with delight, pulling Zazi over to her window to look at a casino. The entrance looked like a giant slot machine.

Further still they travelled, passing over into the business district. The Convoy turned to travel through a green park. The low grass on either side of the winding street gave way to trees and shrubs, here and there. They approached a courtyard with an enormous marble fountain. At the center of the fountain there was a statue of an Ancient One, standing amongst children at play. This figure, whether male or female-Hanu could never tell- was magnificent, yet terrifying. Its pale face had large round eyes and its nose and upper lip joined, sloping downward into a small beak. Its bald head had various colorful nodules protruding from it in an ornate pattern, like a majestic crown. The very tall body was humanoid, but its extremities were cloaked in white feathers. The figure wore a simple tunic.

“Is that a hologram, too, then?” Hanu asked.

“No, that one’s real. It’s actually a historic landmark,” the Scout explained.

Hanu was thoroughly interested. “So what’s historic about it?” he asked.

Addressing the group now, the scout pointed at the statue with an open hand. He looked more like a tour guide than anything else.

“The Fountain of Hope was erected in 2042 as a dedication to the pact that was forged between Humanity and the Ancient Ones. Humanity had nearly wiped itself out through war by 2040, when the Ancient Ones were forced to intervene. But of course, humanity had to agree to receive the help, so they ceased war while they debated the nature of their relationship with the Ancient Ones. After two years of deliberation, humanity finally agreed on the terms for accepting the help. On that day they erected six identical Fountains of Hope- each on a different continent in the world.”

Hanu wondered if the scouts were programmed to just know everything about everything. He was amazed at how much the scout knew, but even still he tried to continue to dislike him.

“There is an inscription at the base of the fountain,” he went on, good-naturedly. “It says, may we walk the path of Ancient wisdom and knowledge, forever as one.”

The passengers craned their necks to see it, but they were already driving away from it. Then Ester spoke for the first time.

“When I’m free, that beautiful fountain is the first place I’ll visit,” she said.

Everyone turned to look at Ester, double checking that it was, in fact, she who had spoken. Ester looked around, her chestnut eyes peeking from behind her curtain of bangs. Then she continued looking out of the window.

“Uh, that sounds like a good plan,” Ms. Felix said, conversationally. “And it’s right along the route to the District. Maybe you can stop here on your way back.”

“Not possible,” said the scout. “Once this group enters the District of Operations you will not be permitted to leave. Well, perhaps as an Easement Request- it is a historic landmark, after all-”

“Easement Request?” Vanessa asked soberly.

An Easement Request was given to people who went for override of their own accord- typically the very old or the very sick. At the Flush, they would try to bribe the patients they took in with an Easement Request so that they would behave on the journey into the District. This boon, whatever wish the person requests, is granted as a final honor.

“You’ve been more than helpful,” Mr. Wolfe said to the scout. But it was already too late. Tui jumped to his feet and rounded on the scout. The adults erected themselves in their seats, ready to pounce.

Chapter Four

"So we are being overridden," he said to the scout, searching his face for confirmation.

The agent blinked several times, as if his artificial eyes needed to be moistened.

"Well, there could be several cases in which the Council grants Easement," he said.

"That's a lie," Tui retorted, somehow looking much older now.

It was if Hanu could feel every individual cell in his body vibrating violently. So they were going to die.

Zazi started shaking her head in denial and Vanessa was yelling profanities. Sadie's nostrils flared. She looked at each of the escorts, jaws clenched, as if deciding who she'd be violent with first. Ester sat calmly, as if she didn't notice what had just transpired.

La was standing up now, too.

"No," he bellowed at Mr. Wolfe, as though that would settle the matter. But somehow Hanu felt like it actually could. For some reason, Hanu stood up, too.

Vanessa stopped screaming just as Mr. Trattonere tackled her. Mr. Wolfe used that distraction to grab La's arms and the scout grabbed Tui. Ms. Felix grabbed for Sadie, and since everyone was grabbing everyone else, Mr. Ervin went for Hanu.

Not altogether unexpectedly, their stomachs dropped. The Convoy was no longer levitating. It propelled forward with a lurch, grinding against the metal street and they sped right into a surveillance tower, exploding into the air. The contents of the Convoy, both people and furniture, tumbled around as it flipped.

The Convoy finally stopped upside down on a sidewalk. Mr. Ervin lost his grip on Hanu, who was in shock. He lay there on the floor, or ceiling, maybe, watching everything as if it were a dream. Sadie pushed the now unconscious Ms. Felix off of her. Blood glued her hair to her face. She limped over to the door and pried it open. Without so much as a word, the twins made a break for it and disappeared into the sunlit street. Sadie pulled Zazi from underneath a table and pushed her through the door, too. Mr. Ervin, moaning under the weight of Mr. Helm, clutched fruitlessly at Vanessa's ankles as she dragged herself through the door next.

Mr. Trattonere was bleeding from his chest, but he was more concerned with programming an alert. He placed the scouts left palm over his own trade interface, pulling up a map on his own screen. After Mr. Trattonere pinpointed their location he sent the alert and the scout opened his mouth, emitting a shrill frequency.

Sadie pulled Hanu to his feet, and was trying to drag him to the door next. "Where's Ester?" He wiped someone's blood from his face and looked for her in the rubble. She was crouched over the control panel.

"We can't leave without Ester!" Hanu yelled over the siren.

"She can handle herself," was all Sadie said as she forced him through the door and ran off down an alleyway. Hanu turned to go back in for Ester, but she was already jumping out of the door behind him. Ester grabbed him by the arm and pulled him away from the Convoy. Then she said one last thing:

"Scatter!"

Chapter Five

Down in the Dumps

One time, at the Flush, Mr. Carlisle gave Hanu a balloon to blow up whenever he was feeling anxious. He was supposed to blow it as big as he could without letting it pop, then let the air out and then do it all over again. The deep breathing and concentration on the task was supposed to be relaxing, or something like that. Hanu blew and blew and blew on that balloon until it was just about ready to pop, but he never felt any less anxious. He eventually just resorted to playing with the thing, which brought more comfort than the actual assignment. Well, one day when he blew it nice and big, he decided to draw a face on it. So he took a marker and put it to the balloon. Obviously he had blown that balloon past its limit, because it immediately popped.

Hanu's lungs felt like that balloon right now as he ran down the sloped alley. He was afraid that if they pressed any harder against his ribs, they would pop. Life at the Flush never really called for strenuous activity, so Hanu wasn't exactly prepared for this type of run. But he knew he was running for his life, so he continued to propel himself forward, despite his protesting lungs.

Chapter Five

Hanu rushed past garbage cans and small bushes, until there was no more alley left. He didn't dare cross the street to get to the next alley, so he followed the city block, keeping cover under the awning that lined the business entrances. At least it would be harder to spot him on the cameras from here, he thought.

The siren was still blaring, a little further away now. Not far enough, though. Hanu's knees began to buckle as he forced one leg in front of the other. More people were filing into the streets now. Was the work day already over? He ran through people- bright bursting blurs against the backdrop of gray- but he didn't slow down. He cleared several blocks this way, turning corners as quickly and randomly as he could, putting as much space as possible between himself and the scene.

His running slowed now. He pushed clumsily through a furry woman who happened to be walking out of the building as he passed, but Hanu dared not stop to help her up. He didn't even to care to yell out an apology over his shoulder. To Hanu, everyone was an enemy right now. The alarm had sounded, and he knew an alert would be sent to everyone's trade.

He cut a corner to run along a tall fence. It looked to be a recycling yard of some sort. There was a break in the fence and it looked just wide enough for him to fit through. Hanu decided to take his chances behind the fence rather than out in the open street, so he side stepped through the gap and dropped himself into a heap of garbage.

And it clearly wasn't the recycle. On impact, the smell of fetid milk and diapers exploded into the air. This pile clearly came from the Child Development Center. But there was no turning back now, he already chose his pile. Instantly, he burrowed his way deeper into the heap. At least nobody would bother to search for him here, he thought.

Hanu wriggled into a good position. His whole body was covered in a fine layer of garbage with his face open to the sky for fresh air. He laid perfectly still, but his heart and mind were racing. Where did everyone else end up? Why was nobody chasing him? Had they already pinpointed him and were just waiting for him to stop so they can come and collect his tired body?

He thought about what he would do if they came for him, and where he would go from here. He waited and wondered, watching the progression of the sun across the sky. Some machinery cranked up in the background. Hopefully this wouldn't be the pile that they chose to incinerate today.

A couple hours later, by the look of the sun, Hanu heard people approaching. Their voices were low at first, then they came closer. There was some shouting, then some shuffling. Then more shouting. They were definitely looking for something. Someone.

Hanu had already thought about his escape plan. He would smear a handful of wet garbage in his pursuer's face and then take off back through the gap in the fence. Fortunately, Hanu had gotten some time to rest; he was ready for more running now. The voices came closer still.

"I'll take this pile over here, Boss. But you know nobody in their right mind would hide out here, right? Smell 'uh knock you clean out," a man said, laughing.

Chapter Five

"Well then I suggest we start lookin' for sleepin' bodies," the boss said with a wheezing laugh. "When they wake up I'll thank 'em personally for that fifty point reward th' Council gave us for lookin'."

"Now don't spend it all at one place," the first man said. And Hanu was surprised to feel the man stepping on top of him, compressing hot diaper juice down his legs. Hanu was increasingly grateful that he didn't have any open cuts.

The man leaned in on Hanu's face. He couldn't have been older than forty, but his leathery skin testified to the days spent out in the hot sun as a garbage man. And he was unusually clean for the profession. His face was smooth shaved and he wore his long brown hair back in a ponytail. The man looked down a crooked nose at Hanu.

"Anything over there, Harris?" the boss yelled.

"Nothin' at all," Harris answered. Then he moved on to the next heap. Hanu let go of the handful of garbage he was grabbing.

He was confused now. He was certain that man saw him; their noses nearly touched. Did the man decide to just give him a break? Hanu wondered if all of the others were so lucky. Settling back into a comfortable position, he continued listening to the voices. There was more shuffling, then shouting, shuffling, then shouting… until the voices eventually ceased.

The sun was low on the horizon now, and the drones had already finished spraying for the evening. Hanu had to think about what he would do. He thought about home. Could he make his way home if he tried? Who could he go to for help getting there? And even if he did make it home, what would mom do? Would she hide him for the rest of his life?

Hanu remembered when his mom finally took him in for psychological testing. It was almost two full weeks after the principals called the meeting at the school. He ran into her room and jumped on her bed one Sunday morning, excited.

"Mommy, guess what! I had a dream, and it was so real," he said. He was so happy that he'd had a dream, and that he actually remembered it that he didn't notice the look of terror on her face. He continued on, bouncing around on her bed.

"In the dream, there were these people that told me that humans were special, that we had all this power," he said, holding his arms out and looking at his muscles, as if he was back in the dream. But he didn't get to finish. Just then, his mom slapped him across the face.

"But…mom," he stammered, confused.

His mom got out of the bed, and he could see the look on her face now.

"How long have you been having dreams? Why didn't you tell me sooner?" she asked in whispered tones. Her voice was urgent as she got dressed.

"I'm on the committee, and my own son isn't even stable. How did I not see it before? I can't keep this a secret," she said, speaking more to herself than him. She rummaged through her drawers, flustered.

"Put on your clothes, Hanu. We're going in for testing today," she said.

Chapter Five

Hanu winced. He couldn't think about it anymore. Home was definitely not an option. He wondered if his father would help. A long time ago, before the Ancient Ones, men and women parented together in the same family. But Hanu wouldn't even know how to find his father. He didn't know the man's name, let alone where he lived or worked.

Whatever the plan, Hanu just had to get up and stretch. Under the cover of darkness, he slowly raised himself out of the trash pile and snuck into the shadows. He felt his way along the fence, looking for another way out that offered a little less exposure from the main street. That, or at least a water faucet. His every move evoked a fresh whiff of hot diaper juice, and after sitting in it for hours he still couldn't get used to the smell.

Hanu continued following the fence, feeling his way past garbage mounds and benches. The ground was still warm from the day's sun.

"You weren't going down without a fight today, huh, kid?" a man said from the shadows.

Hanu stopped in his tracks. He recognized the voice. It belonged to the man who had stepped on him earlier. Harris. He slowly turned around. Harris was sitting on the bench he'd just passed along the fence. He walked right by him and didn't even know it.

"Everyone's looking for you and your buddies. They even gave us all fifty points to ensure an honest effort," he chuckled. The back of Hanu's neck suddenly grew very hot.

"You did a good job taking out that surveillance tower. Made it harder for them to pinpoint your trade in this area," he went on.

"We didn't take it out…I mean, that happened by accident, we weren't…" Hanu said, allowing his voice to trail off.

"Lucky accident," Harris said. "So what cha do to earn a fancy chariot into the District? Hardly nobody gets a chance to see the inside of that castle."

Hanu was reluctant to say anything further. He wondered if the man would chase him if he darted toward the hole in the fence.

"I would've turned you in earlier, if that was my plan. Relax," Harris said.

"Well, we were coming from the Flush… My treatment was failing. Or, I guess I wasn't really trying," Hanu admitted. "They were taking us in for override."

"Man that's some tough stuff there, kid. You mean you hear voices and all that?" the man said.

"Sometimes," Hanu said nervously. It was hard for him to admit the strange things he'd experienced in life because he was so used to getting into trouble for it.

"Well, what kind of voices?" he asked, sitting up in his seat.

Hanu looked around, making sure they were still alone. Not that he could see very far, since the sky offered very little moonlight.

"Um, sometimes they talk to me, kind of telling me that the world is fake... or maybe not as it should be. And then sometimes there are voices that come from people. When people are talking I can hear other voices underneath them. Sometimes they ask for help, or they contradict what the person is saying…it gets really confusing…"

Hanu's voice trailed off again. He didn't even know why he was explaining his psychosis to a complete stranger anyway. This was crazy. Hanu stood there awkwardly as the man thought about what he'd said.

"Sir, if you're not going to turn me in, what is it that you plan on doing? Why did you wait all this time for me to come out?" he asked. Hanu knew he was at the mercy of this man, but he couldn't figure out what in the world he'd want.

"Well, I was curious, honestly. They told us that the escapees were dangerous. But when I saw you in that pile of garbage, I just saw a kid. You're so young…and you looked so terrified. I needed to know your story. And I wanted to see if I could help you," Harris explained.

Someone actually wanted to help. But Hanu couldn't imagine how this man could really be much help, unless he hid Hanu in his apartment for the rest of his life. But he already considered that kind of lifestyle and it just doesn't seem feasible.

"Well how do you plan on helping now, after hearing my story?" Hanu asked.

"Depends on you. What were you planning after you walked out of here?"

Hanu still hadn't figured that one out, though. After all of those hours of racking his brain, he still hadn't even the slightest lead.

"I have no idea," he admitted, sheepishly. "Maybe if I found the others, we could come up with some sort of plan."

Harris got up from the wooden bench and spit on the ground.

"Well, let's get you cleaned up first. Can't take care of business with you smelling like a three day old feces sandwich."

ꟷ

The inside of the service building was cold even though the power, along with the air conditioning, was shut down for the night hours ago. Of course, it didn't help that Hanu had just been hosed down in the yard and was now stripped down to his underwear. Industrial grade soap still frothed in his hair, but he preferred it that way. He was afraid the smell of garbage would linger otherwise.

"Go ahead and dry yourself off as best you can with this," Harris said, throwing Hanu a shirt from his bag. "I know I've got some clothes in my locker that'll do you some good."

Harris crossed the room in the dark and rummaged through a small metal cabinet.

"Do you want to know my name?" Hanu said, twisting his soapy hair in the shirt.

"If you care to share it," the man said.

Chapter Five

"It's Hanu. And you're Harris. Nice to meet you," Hanu said into the darkness. Harris couldn't see it, but Hanu was giving him a pretty good smile.

"Did the voices tell you my name?" Harris asked, laughing at his own wit. Hanu laughed, too.

"No, I learned that fair and square. I heard your boss say it. You know, back when you stepped on me."

"Oh, yeah," Harris chuckled, combing his hand through his hair. "Sorry about that."

Harris shoved a pair of pants and a shirt into Hanu's hands. Hanu put the pants on. They were a little loose, but they did the job. Then he slipped the shirt over his now dry-enough curls.

"Uh, Harris…you never said how you're going to help me," Hanu said. "I know it's up to me, but I have no idea what I should do now. I can't go home, and I can't go back to the Flush. They're looking for me-"

"You said you wanted to find your friends, right?" Harris interrupted, holding an oddly shaped object up to the window to get a better look at it. In the moonlight, Hanu could see that it had smooth surfaces.

"Yeah, but I wouldn't know where to start," Hanu said, gloomily.

"Well, where do the voices say to start?" Harris said.

Hanu laughed. Then he realized Harris wasn't laughing. It was a serious question.

"It doesn't work like that," he said.

“I’m sure it does, actually,” Harris said. “Matter o’fact, I’m sure your friends already told you where they’d be.”

Hanu thought about it. They scattered, just like Ester said. Everyone ran their separate ways. For all he knew they were all captured. He thought about the youngest ones- Zazi and the twins. Were they fast enough to get away? Were they smart enough to hide? He knew Sadie was tough enough to defend herself, but what about Vanessa? And Ester? Where would they go?

“Ester!” he exclaimed, suddenly. It hit him like a sack of bricks. He couldn’t believe it was so obvious. But how could she know?

“That your girlfriend?” Harris teased.

“No, she was on the Convoy with us. It’s something she said right before the crash- ‘when I’m free, that beautiful fountain is the first place I’ll visit’. She went to that fountain. She wants us to meet at The Fountain of Hope!” Hanu said, excited now. Harris clapped his hands together.

“Good, now there’s a start! And to think, you knew it all along,” Harris said. Then he handed Hanu the oddly shaped object. “Put this in your pocket and don’t take it out.”

“What is this?” he asked, rolling it over in his hands. It was pointy at one end.

“It’s going to keep the council from finding you. Scrambles the signal,” he said simply as he walked over to a small closet and pulled out a paper bag. “C’mon, we gotta get outta here.”

“Right now?” Hanu asked nervously. He was starting to feel so comfortable and safe inside the service station, he didn’t want to leave. And so abruptly, too. The thought of going back outside made him feel vulnerable and he just wasn't prepared.

"Well we won't be able to move about so freely once daylight hits. Plus, we'll need to stop at my place for some supplies, but it'll be necessary if you don't want the Council on your back. Better take advantage of the darkness while we can," Harris said.

"And what next? After we find them, Harris?" Hanu asked. He was trying to stall for time, but it was also a good question.

Harris stuffed Hanu's soggy jumpsuit in the bag and mopped up the water from the floor. Then he turned, letting the moonlight streak across his face as he looked at Hanu. Thinking, he chewed on his lip.

"If you kids can't figure out a plan," he said slowly. "I *do* know of a place that you can go. Somewhere safe for people like you."

"Well why didn't you say anything about it earlier instead of beating around the bush?" Hanu laughed nervously.

Harris laughed, too. "Let's go, kid."

Harris put a little water on a potted plant in the window and then headed for the door.

"Haven't watered that baby in days," he said as he led Hanu into a small hallway. They walked quickly toward the glass door on the other end.

"We're gonna take the exit to the delivery yard, but we'll have to walk slowly until we get to those bushes on the other side of the lot. Otherwise that camera over there will pick us up, Hanu, you hear?" he warned.

Luckily Hanu was used to bypassing the cameras this way at the Flush. He was somewhat of a pro at it by now. When Ms. Jones went for her midnight coffee at the nurse's station, he and Akesh would sneak up and down the hallway to each other's rooms to hang out. Sometimes Hanu would keep the book he borrowed from the book closet, and they would stay up all night reading and eating snacks they'd horded. It was the closest thing to a sleepover they would ever have.

"Got it."

The two made their way slowly and awkwardly across the empty lot. Hanu's muscles were tense, despite the slow movements. He was so defenseless in such an open space, and he was ready to take off running at a moment's notice. Little by little, they made their way to the safety of the bushes.

"Harris?" Hanu whispered.

"Yeah, kid?"

"Why are you helping me? You'll be in a lot of trouble if they catch you."

"I'll be in more trouble if I don't."

Chapter Six

Fountain of Hope

It took several hours to get to their destination, but in order to avoid the street lamps, cameras and patrolling scouts they had to take the long way. On top of that, once they got to Harris' apartment he insisted upon taking a shower.

While Harris was washing up Hanu inspected the man's apartment. He had simple brown furniture and shaggy carpeting, and it smelled of oregano. His walls were covered in abstract art, but Hanu was more interested in his very large book collection. The shelf was stuffed to the brim with texts-half of which weren't even written in English. In the window there were all sorts of plants in various sized pots. Some were spiky and others were leafy. He could tell this man liked to grow things the old fashioned way.

When Harris got out of the shower he packed a bag full of spare clothes, foodstuffs, and a small collection of the same oddly shaped objects he'd given Hanu. Hanu returned the one from his pocket, which Harris threw in the pack as well, then they finally set off.

Hanu was tired and sweaty from walking so long in the arid night, but they had made it safely. The two stood in the shadows of a department store that abutted the park. They strained their eyes, looking into the darkness for signs of life. Hanu could make out the place where the fountain was. He could see the silhouette of the statue, watching ominously over the courtyard.

“What now?” Hanu asked.

“We wait. They may not be here, or the place might be watched, so let’s not be too hasty,” said Harris.

Hanu shifted his weight. Then he slumped into the wall, allowing himself to fall into a sitting position. He knew he needed to rest, but he wanted to find the others. He could see a tinge of pink in the sky to the east now, and he knew they were running out of time. He was getting impatient.

“What are we waiting for?” he asked.

“A sign,” said Harris.

Then, in a moment, Hanu stood and turned to the courtyard.

“Haw! Ha-aww!” he called loudly.

“What are you doing?” Harris hissed, covering his mouth.

“I’m sorry, I was following an impulse,” Hanu explained. “I felt like it was the right thing to do.”

Harris pulled Hanu back into the shadows, but that was the sign that was needed. Off to the north, they heard it come back.

Chapter Six

‘Haw Ha-aww!’

Hanu was elated. Someone else had made it. He wondered who it was, and how long they’ve waited.

“Well I guess your impulses know best,” Harris said, pulling him into the park.

The two made their way to the northern end of the green space, right behind where the fountain was. They were sure to hide their movements in the shadows, ducking behind bushes and trees as they approached the courtyard. Occasionally they called out to make sure they were still headed in the right direction, and received a confirmation in return. As they approached the place where the other person should have been Harris stuck out his hand, stopping Hanu in his tracks.

“Let’s approach slowly. This could be a trap,” he warned. “We’ll check this person out first… see if you recognize ‘em.”

“Alright,” Hanu agreed.

They slowly crept along a trellis, eyeing the thicket across the path that separated them from the other person. Hanu stood up to get a better view of the bushes across the way when he caught sight of something else- two scouts a little further up the path.

He dropped his body to the ground with such force he winded himself. He knew they were out looking for the escapees. And he might’ve shook the bush on his way to the ground. They had been caught.

“Scouts!” he hissed, hoping whoever was across the path would hear. Harris crawled up next to him.

"Did they see you?" he asked urgently.

"I think so, but I don't know. They're going to find me," he said, panicking now. His heart was beating too fast. He knew he was going to die. He hadn't had any sleep and now his heart was racing and his body was going to shut down right here in the bushes and the scouts would come and find him.

"Calm down, we need to get out of here quietly," Harris said, digging in his bag. He pulled Hanu under a thick bush a little further from the path.

"Make yourself as little as possible under this bush. Make sure nothing is sticking out," Harris said, and he placed what looked like a rock at the base of the bush.

Hanu's heart continued to race as he hugged the inside of the bush. He was certain that the scouts would follow the sound of its beating straight to him. They were approaching now. He could see their boots on the path, facing where the other person should have been hiding.

"I will conduct a thermal imaging scan," the first scout said.

Hanu's heart was on the ground now. They were sure to find whoever it was that was over there. He held his breath.

"Confirmed," said the other.

Hanu knew that the first scout was holding his arm up, palm open, and sweeping the area. At any moment he would apprehend somebody. There were way too many people in these bushes for them to not find at least one.

From his place in the bush, he could see that the light from the scan had caused the flora in the area to glow in yellows, greens and purples. It would have been a beautiful sight if it hadn't meant certain death for Hanu to be caught in it. He was sure that he couldn't outrun a scout in his current condition.

But then the lights abruptly disappeared.

"Thermal imaging scan complete. No significant sign of life," the scout said.

Hanu exhaled. They hadn't detected anybody.

"Confirmed and recorded. Let us move on to the business district," said the second scout, and they moved on to the west.

The bushes were perfectly still for several minutes after the scouts left. If there were any cameras near, the scouts had activated them.

Harris pulled Hanu out of the bushes, silently signaling for him to follow. Crouching down, they slowly made their way across the path, careful to stay in the shadow cast by the trees. Harris kept watch over the courtyard.

"It's me, Hanu. Are you still there?" he called into the thicket.

Hanu was afraid that whoever it was had been startled by the scouts and left, so he took a more direct approach in case nobody was there to meet with anymore. At least that way they could get it over with and find shelter before the sun was completely up. But then he heard someone behind him.

"Psst!"

Hanu turned and saw her nestled into a bush. Her hair was still slicked with dried blood, but her face was clean.

“Sadie! Where are the others?” Hanu asked excitedly. He knew she was too tough to be caught. He secretly felt like he wouldn’t be surprised if she was the only one who’d made it, but he hoped she would help the others to get somewhere safe.

“Shhh…” she said, quickly putting a finger to her mouth. She had a bloody strip of jumper wrapped around her wrist.

“Sorry,” he whispered. “What happened to you?”

“Don’t worry about it right now. Who’s your friend?” she said.

“Oh, I’m sorry, this is Harris,” Hanu said, introducing them. “He helped me to escape. Harris, this is Sadie.”

“Nice to meet you, Sadie.”

“Pleasure, I’m sure,” she said, eyeing him.

“Where’s Ester? The others?” Hanu asked. He was starting to get a little worried. He’d hoped to find them all there together, but he should’ve known it wouldn’t be so easy.

“Ester and Vanessa are in the damned fountain,” she said, looking very annoyed. “And Zazi said she was going home.”

Then she stood up and dusted off her torn jumper. “The twins got caught,” she sighed.

Hanu wasn’t sure why, but he felt a little guilty for getting away, and he knew that Sadie was also remorseful. He had never seen her look so solemn. She looked over the green space, clenching her jaw.

Harris and Hanu stood up, too, and looked toward the fountain. They didn’t notice the two there before, but sure enough, the girls were splashing each other now as if that's exactly what people should be doing at this time of morning.

"They must be either truly bold or truly certified," Harris said, laughing.

"Watch it now," Sadie said, testily. "And why are you still here, anyway?"

"Woah, I'm on your side!" Harris began, but Sadie had already switched gears. She cut him off.

"Cut the bull, old man, you helped Hanu for a reason. You followed him here to get to us, didn't you? Well guess what, you ain't taking me in!" she said.

"You think you can intimidate me, little girl?" he said, sizing her up.

"I'm just tryin' to get some information. It's not my fault you feel intimidated," she retorted.

Harris laughed.

"You're spicy," he said, laughing again.

Hanu looked around, anxiously. This is exactly the opposite of what he needed right now. Ester and Vanessa heard the commotion and started walking over.

"Harris said there's a place we can go to live. Somewhere safe for people like us," Hanu cut in, trying to stop the argument.

Sadie looked at Harris, thinking. She had that violent look in her eye, but Hanu knew she was debating whether she could trust the man or not.

"We have no other choice. We can't hide in the bushes forever," Hanu reasoned. "I can't go home 'cause my mom will just turn me over, and they'll kill us if they find us. He said it's someplace hidden."

Sadie continued studying Harris. He smiled, knowing he was under her skin.

"Why are you helping us?" she said, and it was Harris' turn to look serious now. The smile faded from his face as he considered his answer.

"I turned my daughter in," he said, nodding his head at the confession. "Reported her when she was six years old. I thought it was the best thing to do for her. I thought they would fix her... send her back happy."

Harris' face was pained. He paused for a moment, looking off into the sunrise now with his tongue in his cheek. "They took her straight to the District for override. I realized after that, that she *was* happy. She knew what others didn't, and she was free. I didn't know what that was or how to address it, so it scared me. It forced me to face the fact that I wasn't free," he admitted.

They stood there in the quiet. Wind blew through the trees, sweeping Sadie's long hair into a frenzy. Her face softened… saddened.

"I'm sorry," Vanessa finally said. They didn't realize she and Ester had arrived to hear his story.

"Come on, Harris. You'll have to get back to work soon, so we need to get going," Ester said, abruptly.

Chapter Six

Harris laughed. “How do you guys put up with her being a know it all?” he asked, thumbing at Ester.

“Well, she actually never really spoke before yesterday, so it was pretty easy,” Vanessa said.

“It sure has been a huge help since then, too,” Sadie added, wrapping an arm around Ester’s neck and pulling her into a hug.

Everyone was so cheerful. Hanu felt like this was going to work- they were going to be safe. Well, everyone except the twins. He felt a pang of guilt for just brushing over them. Nobody offered so much as a moment of silence or anything for them.

“Alright then, if this is everyone, let’s get ready to go,” Harris said, clapping his hands together.

“Guys what about the twins?” Hanu asked.

“We can only control so much, Hanu. Let’s focus on what we can handle, and hope the best for them. We need to get somewhere safe,” Harris said, putting a sympathetic hand on his shoulder.

“So where are we going now?” Vanessa asked.

“The Bathtub Resort. It's in the Entertainment District,” Harris said, and he took off his pack and pulled an assortment of clothes out. “You guys need to change so we can blend in a little better.”

“Right here?” Sadie exclaimed.

"Well, you can get behind a bush, but do it quickly. Suns almost up and people will be heading to work soon. We need to blend in with the morning rush."

Harris turned around quickly now, wide eyed, because Vanessa started throwing off her clothes, mid- instruction. She had often tried to strip down at the hospital, claiming that her uniform was a symbol of oppression, but the staff usually disabled her attempts pretty quickly. It amused Hanu to think that she was finally able to rip the thing off in peace. But then he remembered he should give her some privacy, too, so he also turned around.

"So Harris, we're going to a bar?" Hanu asked, to make sure he understood correctly.

"Yes, it's a bar."

"We're not old enough to get into a bar, though," said Vanessa.

"I am,' Sadie said, proudly. "I just turned sixteen."

"Well, we won't be doing any drinking," said Harris, zipping his backpack back up and throwing it over his shoulder. "Come on. I'll explain everything on the way."

ꕥꕥꕥꕥꕥꕥꕥ

Harris knocked on the tiny door of the Bathtub Resort three times and walked away to where everyone was casually standing behind a holographic marquee.

"Look natural," he said to the gang.

Hanu wondered how a group of random teenagers, all wearing helplessly mismatched clothes, could look natural on this street, but he tried anyway. He stood up straight and pretended to be very interested in the marquee. It read:

'Weekend Special: Any drink in the house, 1 point. 3 hours Holo-company, 12 points. Best deal in town.'

And it must've worked, because the people passing in the street did a good job of ignoring them. The door to the bar unlocked with a definitive click. Everyone looked up.

"Come on," said Harris, and he walked in.

Hanu felt uneasy about walking into a bar, but he followed apprehensively anyway. Sadie helped him along by shoving him past the threshold.

"Calm down, Sadie, we're not even drinking," he said, playfully.

"*You're* not drinking," she retorted.

The bar was quite large on the inside. It was one big square, dimly lit by neon signs, and had an assortment of empty tables dotting the room. There were three pool tables in the back, along with a very large bathtub, which held a bubbling liquid.

"Can we get some pool balls?" Vanessa asked, excitedly, running up to one of the tables.

"Won't be here long enough, Vanessa," Harris said, locking the door behind them.

"What is a bar open so early for?" Hanu asked.

"Well I don't actually open up 'til 7:30, but I'm here all night to do different business related stuff," said the barkeep.

Hanu jumped. He hadn't noticed the round man sitting in the far corner of the place.

"But you'd be surprised at the amount of wretched souls that drag tail in here that early for a morning pick-me-up! Ain't that right, Harris?" he said, slapping the table and laughing.

"Those are the ones who usually end up ordering The Harriet," Harris said, smiling fondly. And they laughed together. The gang looked at each other with raised brows.

"So's that what we're ordering today, then, huh?" he said, looking at each of them in turn. "When we talked yesterday there was only one. What happened?"

"Well, you know, Toni…" Harris chuckled.

"These kids need some lemon with that?" Toni asked.

"All of them, yes," Harris said. His demeanor was matter of fact, as he ordered drinks for the bunch.

"Look kinda young to me," Toni said.

Hanu was both confused and worried. He was definitely under-aged, and he definitely didn't want the Harriet- especially since they were supposed to be running for their lives. This was wrong on several counts.

He looked at Ester to gauge the appropriate level of alarm he should be feeling. Maybe she would give him some indicator of just how bad the situation really was. But her expression was just as placid as ever as she took a seat in one of the chairs near the bar.

"They came from the flush. Implanted their trades early," Harris said.

Chapter Six

Toni got busy behind the counter. He pulled out a box from underneath the bar and opened it up. From where Hanu stood, he could see a lever of some sort sticking out of it. The man tapped the lever rhythmically, and it made a beeping noise. Then he pulled out a cocktail class and poured a brown liquid into it.

"On the house, Harris," he said. Then he walked to the kitchen doors.

"Be right back… gonna get that lemon ready," he said as he disappeared through the doors. Hanu rounded on Harris. He would have to be the voice of reason here.

"Harris, now's not the best time to be drinking," he said urgently. "We really need to be going."

"Speak for yourself," said Sadie, and she picked up the glass of brown liquid. "He said it was on the house." And she tipped the glass, pouring it all into her mouth at once.

"Aaaargh!" she yelled, spitting the stuff onto the floor and countertop. "This is disgusting, how do people drink this?"

The gang laughed as she gagged.

"Well first off, they drink it one sip at a time," Harris said, taking the glass from her. He put it on the counter and took his backpack off. "Come on guys, gather around. We need to eat and discuss some things."

Harris took a seat at Esters table and opened his bag, pulling out bread and cheese. Everyone grabbed for the food at the same time. Hanu wondered if the rest of them had been lucky enough to find food while they were all separated, but by the looks of it, they hadn't.

“I need to explain what’s going to happen,” he said. Everyone sat, quietly chewing.

“You’re going to the Underground. Lots of people have moved there for various different reasons since these Ancients showed up on our planet. Whatever reason they find refuge there, there is one thing that is agreed upon, and this is the first law: the Underground is to remain hidden at all cost,” he said darkly.

“For this reason, the first thing we’ll do is remove those trades they put in your arms. The rest of the world cannot know where the Underground is, and those things will lead them right to it.”

Everyone looked around, nodding agreeably.

“I will tell you now,” he continued. “It’s not an escape to a magical fairytale castle where you’ll live happily ever after.”

“Good, cause I ain’t no princess,” Sadie said. And Harris cut her off, raising his voice a little.

“There, you will be pulling your own weight. You help to grow food. You feed and water the animals-”

“Animals?” Vanessa interrupted.

“Shhhh!” Hanu said. He was sitting on the edge of his seat, anxious to hear more.

“You take your turn caring for the children, and you learn a trade,” he continued, but Hanu cut him off this time.

“What do you mean, learn a trade?” he asked.

"I mean you learn to do something that contributes to society- furniture making, farming, healing, and storytelling- those kinds of things. It's sometimes harsh, living in secret. But it's a close-knit community. You will rely on each other to survive. You learn together, you celebrate together, you cry together and you heal together. It's radically different from life up here," he warned.

Hanu felt tears welling in his eyes. It sounded like something he could get used to. Especially if people like Harris were there. He hardly knew the man, but Harris talked to him like he was just Hanu- not Hanu, the mental health patient, or Hanu, the kid who doesn't know what he's talking about.

He could imagine the world Harris was describing, where everyone grew together, and he knew it was real. He felt like he'd been there before, and was simply returning. His eyes were stinging. A tear streaked down his cheek, but he didn't care.

"Do people ever change their minds, Harris?" Ester asked. "You know, after living in the Underground? Do they ever come back?"

"You go to the Underground to find refuge... *freedom*. Once you find that, you don't want to come back," Harris replied. "Besides, if the Ancient Ones want you dead, you're dead. There's no coming back for people like you."

"How do we get there?" Vanessa asked.

"It will take some time to get there," Harris said. "First you'll need to go to deprogramming."

And at this they looked at Harris with furrowed faces, torn from the reverie.

“It sounds… *unpleasant*,” Harris began.

“It sounds painful,” Vanessa interjected.

“Look guys, whatever it sounds like, you need to go there first. Everyone goes there to make the transition. It’s to make sure you’re okay and to make sure the Underground stays secret and safe. No pain involved,” Harris explained.

Everyone looked at each other again. Hanu watched Ester. He didn't know how, but she seemed to know the right thing to do. He decided he would go to Deprogramming if Ester went. It would be nice if Harris were there, too, he thought.

“So why don’t you come to the Underground with us?” Hanu asked.

“I have to go to work,” Harris said, matter-of-factly.

“Well, run away.”

“One day I will, Hanu, but for now I need to help others find it first. I kinda have a knack for it,” he said, leaning back in his chair and giving a little wink. Hanu smiled, grateful that Harris was the one who caught him hiding in that garbage pile.

“So how do we remove the trades?” Ester asked, looking at her wrist.

“Glad you asked,” Harris said as Toni walked back out of the kitchen holding a small pot. He walked through the liquid Sadie spit out and almost slipped.

Chapter Six

"What's this all over the floor?"

ஒஒஒஒஒஒஒஒ

Inside the kitchen there was a large table covered with a white sheet. Various knives, bottles and cotton balls were lined neatly on a small tray, along with a small velvety box.

"Alright gang, did Harris tell you what we're doing?" the man asked, looking around. He was pretty old. The hair on his head had relocated to the inside of his ears and his neckline, but his brown eyes were vibrant. Hanu could tell that he enjoyed helping people in this way.

"I think he left the details for you to explain," said Hanu, looking at Harris nervously. He wasn't too concerned about it earlier, but now that he saw the layout he knew that whatever the process was, pain would be involved.

"Well I think you can tell it won't be pretty," he said, gesturing toward the tools. "So I won't sugarcoat it."

"Thank you," Sadie said. To the point, just like she liked it.

"First you'll have to drink some of this. It's a painkiller- my own special blend," he explained. "It kicks in instantly, but only lasts so long, so I'll immediately remove the trade with these tools. If you don't move, it takes two minutes."

"What if you do move?" Ester asked.

"You die," he said simply. And he didn't bat an eye before moving on. "Then I'll bandage you up and you'll have to drink this one."

Toni opened up the small velvety box and pulled out a small vial for the group to see. It contained a yellow liquid, and Hanu could swear that he heard a chittering noise coming from it. It was as if the liquid were alive.

"This will disable the nanotechnology in your bloodstream. This is the lemon," he explained. "I'll tell you now, this is the worst part. You'll know it's working by the excruciating pain you feel right after downing it."

"I ain't got no nanotechnology in my blood," Sadie said, shaking her head.

"We all do," Harris said. "It's released from the trade when they put it in you. It's kinda like the maintenance crew for the trade, but it also happens to be traceable through GPS and other locating systems, so all of it has to go."

"Wait," Hanu said, changing the subject. "If that's the case, why haven't they tracked us all down yet? We've been all over this city and not once was anyone on our tail. Why is nobody looking for us now?"

Harris pulled his backpack off once more and grabbed his assortment of oddly shaped objects. He gently placed them on the table- four geometric figures and two rocklike objects.

"They *are* looking for you, but I told you, these tools scramble signals. Before that, when you were in the pile of garbage they couldn't locate you the traditional way cause the nearest surveillance tower was blown, so they went to doing heat scans. You were just fortunate enough to jump into the hottest pile of garbage on the lot," Harris said.

"So right now our signals are gone? You mean once you showed up at the fountain our signals were gone too?" Sadie said.

"Yeah, the more you carry the broader the range. But I don't know what kept you ladies safe before that," he said, eyeing Vanessa and Ester. He was no doubt thinking about them playing in the fountain.

"I knew it was safe to relax a little once you guys showed up. We had spent all night taking turns on guard duty," Ester said. "But really, the twins gave the scouts a really hard time before they were caught. So while everyone was focused on the part of town they destroyed, we kind of slid by."

Hanu felt another pang of guilt. He wondered if they were alive right now. But Toni broke his thoughts before he could get too disheartened.

"Look, guys, reminisce on the way to Deprogramming. We need to get this thing going…bar opens in forty-five minutes," he said. "Who's first?"

Harris walked back through the doors to keep an eye on the front as Sadie sat down across from the man. She unwrapped her arm. "I'll go first. This should be easy enough- I did half the work for you," she said, revealing a bloody gash on her wrist. Toni was incredulous.

"I'm surprised you're not dead. You know there's a major artery in this arm, right?" he said, inspecting the gash.

"In that case, I'm surprised I'm still alive, too," she said, smirking.

"So did Harris tell you about the whole process? You know, Deprogramming first and all that?" he said conversationally.

"Yeah, it'll be fun," she said, wincing.

"Looks like you got the trade," he said, and then he bandaged her arm. Then he scooped a ladle of the painkiller up for her. "Drink this, anyway. It'll help with the next part."

Sadie drank it in one gulp and then held her hand out for the vial, which Toni was uncorking. The liquid was definitely effervescing now. Then she drank that one down, too.

"At least this stuff is sweet," she said. "Better than that crappy drink you served up there."

Then a moment later she stood up, clutching her stomach. She looked alarmed.

"This won't kill me, right?" she asked.

Hanu looked at Sadie. Beads of sweat were welling up on her forehead and nose, and her nostrils flared as she tried to slow her breathing. He'd never seen her like this before, she was genuinely afraid. And that made him nervous, being as he would be drinking that stuff, too.

"Nobody ever died from it, sweetheart. Some people do get diarrhea though, so the toilets through there if you need it," he said casually, pointing toward the backdoor. "We gotta keep this moving, kids. Time's not on our side."

Hanu hesitated. He wanted to see how far this went with Sadie. So Vanessa went ahead and took her turn, sitting in front of the man. She drank her dose of the first medicine. Then Hanu had to look away when Toni picked up the knife. He didn't want to see it until after his own turn.

It went quickly. She didn't make a sound until after she drank the yellow liquid.

"Tastes like lemon!" she said, excitedly. Then her expression immediately changed. "Is it supposed to burn?" she asked, pushing back in her chair slowly.

"Yes," Toni said, beckoning for the next person. He dabbed his forehead with a small cloth.

Hanu looked at Sadie again. She was silently crying, eyes and fists clenched. It looked as though she was using all the restraint she had to not punch something. Vanessa began bouncing up and down on the balls of her feet and looking around, possibly for that bathroom. He decided that since they weren't immediately dying, he would go ahead and take his turn.

It's not that bad, he told himself as he drank the medicine. And he was right. Hanu only felt a slight pressure on his forearm. The surgery lasted no more than a minute, then Toni was handing him an uncorked vial.

"Do it all in one gulp," he advised.

As he tipped his head back he saw Vanessa, blubbering quietly with her head in her hands. The liquid was thick in his mouth, but it did taste like lemon. As he swallowed it down, though, his hands started shaking. He was anticipating the pain.

By the time it actually hit he was doubled over. His heart was already racing, and now his gut was being ripped open. The pain radiated from his stomach to his extremities, then he broke into a sweat. He was in a full on panic.

"I'm dying," he said out loud. "I'm too young… my body can't handle this," he stammered. Then he heard the voices.

'Turn yourself in... You won't die if you just turn yourself over to the Ancient Ones... This man poisoned you, but the Ancients know how to stop it...'

"Where did you get that stuff from?" he asked. "They made a mistake. It's... not..."

Hanu couldn't get his words together. He just had to leave. He pushed through the kitchen doors and ran straight into Harris.

"Harris, I'm sorry, I have to go. I have to get help. I'm turning myself in," he said, trying to escape the man's grasp.

Harris grabbed Hanu, hugging him and patting his back. Hanu felt like a baby, but it was just what he needed. He reverted back to his younger self now, allowing himself to be held. His racing thoughts started to calm. He stopped fighting.

"Hanu these guys program us from birth to be dependent on them. They tell you what to think and how to act. It's a learned reaction to need them in a tough situation," he said in Hanu's ear. "Don't worry, we have a lot of knowledge and experts on our side, too. You won't die. As a matter of fact, it's almost over, okay?"

"Okay," Hanu said, quietly, grabbing Harris now. "Don't let me go until it's over."

After a while Toni burst through the kitchen doors. Hanu pushed Harris away from him. He already felt bad enough for panicking and running out- he didn't want anyone seeing him coddled.

"The girls are done in here, Harris. Ellie just showed up, too."

Chapter Six

"Come on, Hanu. It's time to get out of here," Harris said.

They walked back into the kitchen where the girls were sitting now, bitter faced. The refrigerator was pulled away from the wall, exposing a hidden door, which Toni was unlocking. It revealed a small room. All three walls were lined with wine racks, filled to the top with a variety of bottles.

"I call this my secret stash. It's where the journey really starts, eh, Harris?" Toni said loudly, slapping Harris on the back. Harris stepped in and pulled a bottle of wine off of the rack.

"You get way too excited about all of this stuff, Toni, you know that?" he said, smirking. Then he flipped a switch on the wall behind where the bottle was and lifted the whole rack, pulling hard. The whole wall moved, opening to reveal a staircase descending to a fowl smelling tunnel. A very pale woman in a brown cloak was climbing the stairs.

"Hi everyone," she said, giggling nervously. She was a very tall woman, and looked to be a little older than Toni. Her blonde hair was pulled into a ponytail on the side of her head, but Hanu could see that it was thinning. Despite being older, though, she had a very bubbly innocence about her round face.

"So these are our runaways?" she said, whispering 'runaways' loudly behind her hand. Hanu wasn't sure why she was whispering, being as everyone here was in on it. Ellie looked around, smiling, as everyone greeted her in turn.

"Everyone this is Ellie," Harris said, introducing them. "She's a ferry."

Vanessa snickered loudly at this, and everyone turned around.

"Not a *fairy*, with magic sprinkles, a *ferry* like something that takes people from one point to another," Harris clarified. "She'll be taking you to deprogramming."

"Oh."

Ellie smiled and waved enthusiastically at her introduction. "So did you message Paula?" she asked Toni, nodding her head vehemently for confirmation. Hanu wasn't sure if he should trust this lady with taking them where they needed to go. She seemed… off. But Harris trusted her, and besides, there was no going back now.

"When they arrived, 'bout thirty minutes ago," Toni said. "She's expecting you, though. I'll let her know you're on your way once you guys get going."

"If you guys move quickly you should be there by six or so this evening," Harris said, handing Sadie a bag of food. "Now don't forget to eat, and when you get there you'll be able to get plenty of rest, so don't worry about that. They'll take good care of you."

Hanu was suddenly sad to be leaving Harris. He thought about his daughter, and how miserable Harris must be to have lost her. He wondered if Harris was punishing himself by staying here and helping others escape. Maybe he was making it up to her by doing so.

"Thank you for helping us, Harris," he said. "One day we'll see you in the Underground, okay?"

"Sure thing, kid. I'll look out for you," he said, smiling. Then Ellie clapped her hands together.

“Alright, group, let’s move out! I’m so excited for this adventure. You know, I make this walk all the time, but it’s always so fun seeing new faces,” she went on, smiling brightly and nodding her head. Then she thanked Toni and Harris and started walking down the stairs, gesturing for everyone to follow.

Hanu took one last look around. Two days ago life was perfectly normal. Well, as normal as it could be for someone like him. And now he was walking away from everyone he cared about and everything he knew. Life will never be the same from here on out for him.

He turned around and followed Ellie down the stairs.

Chapter Seven

Deprogramming

Almost a full day later the group started its ascent. The tunnel was elevating, and they could see a narrow stairway that ended with a large door. Light emanated from behind it, illuminating the path in long streaks. The children's eyes had become so accustomed to the dim lamps along the tunnels walls that the doorway was like radiant beacon.

"We're here, right?' Hanu asked hopefully.

Even Sadie was too tired to have a bad attitude. "Please tell me we're done when we get up these stairs," she said.

Up until this point, they had stopped asking Ellie questions because she would often stop walking to over-explain. Then they were stuck listening politely while she prattled on and on. By the end of her rants they would forget what the question was, let alone if it had been answered. If the tunnel didn't have so many off shooting side tunnels they probably would have just went on ahead without her.

But the children were desperate this time, and in need of some reassurance. Not having slept in quite a while, they were at their limit.

Chapter Seven

"This is the last stretch, I promise," Ellie said, smiling cheerfully. "That staircase leads to Deprogramming. It's just a big cave, though, so don't expect anything too fancy."

And then she stopped again. "Alright, before we get all the way up there I'll have to warn you guys- Paula's one tough cookie. I mean, I'm not trying to say anything bad about anyone, you know….but, anyway, we all are different, and all… So, Paula-"

But Hanu stopped listening. He was looking at Ellie now in the dim lamplight. She had been so energetic this whole trip, even as they rested. Back at the Bathtub Resort she looked to be pretty old, though. He wondered how she was so lively all the time. He could see the lines around her mouth and eyes, exaggerated by the light. He wondered if she was so pale because she spent all of her time in this dark tunnel. And maybe that's why she was so… *talkative*. But still, she was very pleasant.

"So just remember to be respectful, and just follow your instincts is all you have to do," she continued nervously. And then she started walking again. "Well come along, now. We really have to stop stopping like this, guys!"

Hanu continued walking, laughing to himself.

"This lady is nuts," Vanessa whispered as she passed him, then she broke out into hysterical laughter. Then a raspy voice came from just ahead on the stairway.

"You morons are lucky I didn't call for the tunnel to be collapsed. What's the hold up?"

They hadn't noticed the woman at the bottom of the staircase. She stopped just close enough to talk to them, holding both hands behind her back.

"Oh, hi Paula! It was my fault, of course… well, and then we had to rest, you know," she explained as she twisted a sleeve of her robe.

Paula stood on the bottom step, looking at them with inscrutable eyes.

"Just hurry up before I change my mind about collapsing the tunnel," she sighed. Then she turned on her heels and started climbing the stairs. The group followed Paula silently for the rest of the walk. She moved rather quickly, so they had to push themselves to keep pace.

When they reached the top they were surprised to see that the large cavern was quite hospitable. A large pool took up the majority of the ground, leaving room only for a long table surrounded by chairs. Hanu could see several other doorways along the shore of the pool. They probably led to other secret entrances like the one at the Bathtub Resort, he thought. Stairs were built along the cave wall, giving access to various cavities enclosed by stone or glass.

"Woah, this is amazing!" Hanu exclaimed, looking at the waterfall on the other side of the pool. Above the rocks was a clear statue. It looked exactly the same as the tools Harris used to scramble their signals. It had a large base with a pointed top. But this one had a metal wire coiled around it. Hanu wondered if it was used to keep this place hidden.

"Can we drink this water?" Ester asked, looking into the pool.

Chapter Seven

"Not just yet, kiddos," Paula said. "First I'll tell you how Deprogramming works, then we'll have to lay down some ground rules."

Paula wore a green tunic over white pants and her wavy hair fell down her copper cheeks like waterfalls. In the light of the cavern Hanu could see that she might have been even older than Ellie. Her face was kind, but stern. Hanu didn't need the warning that Ellie had given- he wouldn't have messed with this woman out of sheer common sense.

"Uh, excuse me, Paula," Ellie interjected. "Don't forget to let them know we'll be feeding them. You know, they're young and… well, they should be good and hungry by now."

"Of course, as long as I can speak without interruption," Paula continued. "My name is Paula. I won't bother with your names because I will forget them. You'll have to excuse me, but too many people come through here for me to bother. I'll learn them eventually, as you'll be here for six days, at least. You're obviously here either for refuge or because of an awakening to the treachery of our current situation up there. Either way, you will have to shed your old ways of thinking and step into some truths. If you turn your attention to the waterfall-" and she gestured toward the pool, "-you'll see what is called a pyramid- they don't teach you about these in school anymore. Not only does this act as a power generator, but it draws in disharmonic energy and converts it into a higher frequency. In essence, it creates a healing space for everything around it. Negative programming and thought forms will be released, if that's what you agree to do."

"Excuse me, but what do you mean, if that's what we agree to do?" Hanu interrupted.

"It means you don't have to be deprogrammed if you don't want to. It's your choice. But your being here is evidence enough that you do not wish to continue living under the regime of our current invaders, so I don't see you opposing the opportunity to shed the thought forms they have implanted within you," she explained impatiently.

Hanu was still confused, but he didn't want to inconvenience her by asking more questions, so he was relieved when Sadie spoke up.

"I'm sorry, but what are thought forms?" she asked.

"A simple thought form is a collection of presuppositions and ideas that define a group's thinking. Naturally, it is created and agreed upon by a group," Paula explained. "But the Ancient Ones, who harbor deep knowledge of the mind, implant thought forms within humans that serve their own best interest. Your thoughts and desires become what the Ancient Ones wish for you to think and desire."

Hanu thought about his reaction earlier at the Bathtub Resort. The voices he had heard- *'you won't die if you just turn yourself over to the Ancient Ones... This man poisoned you, but the Ancients know how to stop it...'*

"You will be shedding those programs that do not serve your true selves, and it requires nothing more than you to be willing to do so. During your stay here, I will be determining if you are safe enough to go to the Underground. We've had artificial humans and other spies attempt to find our location in the past, so we can't be too careful," she said, but then she paused too long, giving Ellie an opportunity to interrupt.

Chapter Seven

"Um, Paula, I just want to remind you… I mean, are you going to tell them about the safety rules, you know-" she started.

"Just as soon as I can continue, yes, Ellie. I will tell them about the safety rules," she said, walking over to the staircase now.

There was a black box on the wall that looked like a cabinet. She unlocked it to reveal a rather large keypad with a blinking button. "Now our main priority here is to keep the Underground safe. Thousands of people rely on our vigilance and ability to keep them hidden. So these are our non-negotiable procedures in case we are invaded or otherwise attacked. First, any intruder in our tunnels will both trigger an alarm and unlock this box. It is everyone's first duty to come to this box and activate document destruction by hitting the blinking button, which will cause the data room-" and she pointed to one of the doors on the opposite shore of the pool. "-to explode, destroying all of our evidence. Then, we must escape through that tunnel." And she pointed to another door underneath the stairway. Hanu looked at the keypad, putting the procedures in his memory.

"And one last thing," she added. "If we are captured you must kill us before they take us away. You have not been to the Underground, but Ellie and I have. They could glean valuable information from our minds if we are captured."

And now the children looked at each other, wide eyed. They were mortified.

“Good stuff, Paula,” Ellie said, mock clapping and nodding excitedly. “Now come on guys, let’s eat and then I’ll show you to your rooms. We need some rest!”

Later on that night, after everyone ate and washed up, Hanu found himself in his room. Vanessa and Sadie were paired into one, and he and Ester shared another. The living quarters were incredibly cool and dry compared to the humidity of the cavern. There were four beds and a dresser, and not much else. It was the most inviting sight he’d seen in days.

Hanu dropped onto his bed, face first, and sank into the soft herringbone comforter. He watched as Ester raised a hand to the glass wall, palm forward, and looked out over the pool.

“Ester?” he said.

“What is it, Hanu?” she asked, still looking at the pool.

“How do you know things? I mean, how can you tell things are going to happen? Like meeting at the fountain, and about Harris?” he asked. Ester thought for a while, stroking her dark hair.

“I don’t know how I know, I just know. Sometimes when I look at someone, I can tell what they’re thinking or what’s going to happen to them,” she explained. “For instance, when we got into the Convoy at the Flush, I knew we’d be escaping that day. I didn’t actually know we would be meeting at the fountain, though. I felt like we needed to stick together, so I said something about it, hoping everyone would know when the time was right.”

"If you know so much, then why are you so quiet all the time? You could really help people," he said.

"Well, talking too much is what landed me at the Flush in the first place. And then the psychiatrist kept giving me more drugs, so I just learned to stay quiet about those things. Eventually, I stopped talking at all, because why talk with others if it can't be authentic?" she said, getting in her own bed.

"Ester?" Hanu said once more. He could feel himself drifting to sleep, but he had to know. "Will we be okay?"

"I hope so, Hanu," she said quietly.

And they fell asleep.

ಌಌಌಌಌಌಌ

The next day Paula called a meeting. The gang dragged themselves down the stairs, feeling the full brunt of the nonstop workout they'd had in the last couple days.

"Good afternoon, sleepyheads," Paula said. "We'll have some breakfast after a while, when Ellie wakes up. But first, there are some basic truths I want you to start chewing on right away. If any of you happen to still harbor piercing admiration for the Ancient Ones and their pets, the Council, you will unfortunately be disillusioned right now. I am going to share with you a little history of our planet."

Paula gestured for them to have a seat at the long table. There was a very large and very tattered book pulled out. Its spine was about six inches thick, and if its paper was ever white, it had turned to a dark brown color now. The book had no title or author on its leather cover.

Deprogramming

Paula opened the book to the first page. It showed a picture of a tall, pale birdman ushering humans into a temple.

"This is the Tome of the Earth. This one is merely a replica of the original, which is kept in a secret place in the Underground, but it contains all of the wisdom and history accumulated over recorded time," she said.

"Are we going to read the whole thing?" Hanu asked, leaning in to look at the picture. There was very small handwriting underneath it.

"No, that would take forever. I'm going to point out the most important details and then you all will be free to peruse it at your leisure. Let's begin," she said, smoothing out the page. "The Ancient Ones, are indeed ancient. They never lied about that. As early as seven thousand years ago they have been materializing in our world for a time. They always come during times of strife to reel humanity back in from the brink of self-destruction, and humanity is grateful to have a higher being to follow. The Ancient Ones claim to be our creators and teach humans how to live properly in their eyes, and they leave an explicit set of rules to follow upon their departure. Sometimes they ask for blood sacrifices and sometimes they give us rules on diet or societal structure. Every time they leave, though, they make sure that the ones they have groomed to control us-and their progeny- continue to uphold those rules."

"You mean the Council?" Hanu interrupted.

"Exactly," Paula said.

Chapter Seven

"And in the past, Kings and Queens, and Emperors, and Pharaohs right?" Sadie said. "They were telling us in school how they were appointed by the Gods."

"Yes, that is all true," Paula continued. "Now ordinarily this wouldn't be such a bad thing, but they are not who they say they are. They claim to come from different planets in the galaxy- and they may- but it looks more like they are coming from a different dimension. You see, even when they aren't walking amongst us, they are able to influence us mentally- just as they do now. They are a parasitic race that can both inspire us to make beautiful art-" and she turned to a page with a colorful mosaic. "-or terrible weapons," she said, turning to another page with a violently orange mushroom cloud. This illustration had a description along the bottom.

"These beings have been historically known as the offspring of Apate or the Army of Set. They've also been called Titans, Fallen Angels, or Nephilim. Whatever their names, we are sure of one thing: They have been trying to take over our planet for centuries using nuclear war. It's the same pattern in each epoch," Paula went on.

"Why do they want to take over Earth? And what's wrong with their planet?" Hanu had a million questions. "And why do they keep getting us to destroy our planet if they want it for themselves?"

"They abandoned their own planet," Paula said, flipping to another page. This one contained a picture of a humanoid figure with various colored dots lined along its center, and it was shrouded in different colored spheres. "The natural progression of intelligent life forms is to grow mentally, physically, emotionally and spiritually- all in balance. These beings neglected their emotional and spiritual bodies for a great deal of their species' evolution, and so they became devoid of them. It's very important for you to understand that a planet and its intelligent life are one. They've compromised their planet, and now they need a new one to live on."

"Well that still doesn't answer why they would make us bomb our own planet," Ester said.

"And why don't they just kill us all off and take over for good?" Sadie added.

The children leaned in closer to Paula. This was the history lesson they never got at the Flush, and they were thoroughly enthralled.

"Well, if you think about it, I just told you why they won't kill us off," Paula said, pointing at the picture. "A planet and its life forms are one. If the intelligent life is altered, so is the planet itself. If the intelligent life is extinct, so is the planet. They only wish to alter us, for control, but not completely eradicate us, because our planet will also die."

Then Paula took a minute to find another page in the book. This one had a diagram of a smaller mushroom cloud with even more tiny little words littering the page.

"They cause us to drop nuclear blasts specifically. Every epoch they inspire scientists and military leaders to create the same weapon of war. The military uses it to wipe out the enemy, unknowing that what they are really doing is creating a way for the Ancients to enter our reality. The energetic output blasts a hole through interdimensional space, allowing them to enter our dimension in physical form. This blast terraforms our atmosphere for a time, but they cannot survive for more than a couple hundred years here. As of late they have been working hard to keep our atmosphere in their ideal conditions- hence the spraying in our atmosphere and weather controlling devices. I'm sure you poor kids have never heard of rain until a few days ago. I heard it was a beautiful sight," she said, gazing longingly over at the pool.

"When the water was falling from the sky," Ester told Hanu, who was the only one looking quite confused. Apparently the girls knew that that was rain, and that it was a normal weather pattern, because they were all nodding their heads.

"Killing people off with the blast is, unfortunately, a clever tactic for them though," Paula continued. "It would serve to kill most of the peaceful people, leaving only war minded individuals. It's easier to control the competitive and war-wounded types. Those are the ones who believe that humanity is nothing more than animals that need to be caged by a higher being."

Then Paula flipped through the pages, deciding which one she'd discuss next. There was an occasional, you guys are too young for that, or that's too scary to think about, which made Hanu nervous. He wanted to glimpse the photos but didn't want to be stuck trying to push images out of his mind. His imagination already wandered too far as it was. He did, however, accidentally glance a shot of an Ancient One whose chest cavity was opened. The page was titled, Basic Make-Up of an Ancient.

"Here we go," she finally said, pointing to an illustration of the human brain. "So how do they control us? They use media, schooling, and drugs. At the beginning of the first real influential war before the Ancients arrived this time around, some idiot created the television. This device was just a box that you had to look into and it would send you messages. There would be an overt message, such as “our economy is worse than it’s ever been. Lend a helping hand to a good neighbor.” But then there was a covert message, subliminally sent directly to your brain, such as “our economic problems were orchestrated by Jewish people. We need to get rid of them.” That, in conjunction with other mind controlling devices worked well enough to kill millions of Jewish people in that country.”

Hanu thought about the news anchors that visited the social room every morning and the movies that they would occasionally watch at the Flush. What messages could they be sending to the patients?

“Then there are the various drugs in our food, water and air that shut down both our higher levels of thinking and our foresight. Those drugs, in conjunction with the frequencies they're shooting off from these towers, keep us content with the state of things as they are,” she continued. “As far as schooling, you spend your days memorizing useless bits of information that have no actual practicality in the real world.”

“And that’s why I never did my homework!” Sadie said, laughing. Hanu and the others frowned. Apparently they had always done theirs.

“Neither did I,” Paula said, smiling at Sadie.

“Okay, so the Ancient Ones are trying to take over our world, but they haven’t figured all the kinks out yet,” Hanu said, sitting back in his chair. “Why did they bother building the mental hospitals? Why don't they just kill the ones who are malfunctioning?"

"What do you mean, malfunctioning?" Paula asked, sitting up.

"You know. I hear voices and Ester know things, and Sadie has... well I don't know what's wrong with Sadie except she gets mad a lot. And Vanessa… well…" he gestured toward Vanessa as a whole, who was looking at the pyramid and tracing loops in the air with her finger. She wore a gratified smirk.

"We ended up at the Flush because we don't fit in," Ester helped.

"Well Hanu, haven't you been listening this whole time?" Paula asked impatiently. "After a while the tricks they pull stop working and people start waking up. It seems like you all are insane because that is what they're telling you, but you've returned to what humans are supposed to be at this time in our planets evolution. You all have access to the fourth dimension in some way or another."

"Fourth dimension?" Ester raised a brow.

Paula grumbled something about the public education system being worthless as she rubbed her temples.

"Think of dimensions as parallel worlds that exist alongside ours. As we journey through time, we evolve and become higher dimensional beings. We change. We become more connected- to our world and to each other."

Hanu shifted in his seat, trying to absorb Paula's words. "So when we have access to the fourth dimension we hear and see things that nobody else can?"

"Yes, you have greater access to your intuition, but most importantly, you have greater manifesting power. So with the right knowledge and physical abilities you would be capable of manipulating your environment. You'd be capable of dispelling these creatures for good."

Paula flipped ardently to another page in the book. This one had a picture of a strand of DNA.

"The Ancients wouldn't be as popular with the general public if they were getting rid of children left and right, so they try to 'rehabilitate' you through aggressive drug therapy. These drugs shut down portions of the brain and body that are evolving beyond their ability to control. So occasionally they take a few patients for genetic experimentation so that they can create new drugs that counter our evolving bodies. You children are powerful, and don't you forget that. Why else would they want to kill you? Why else would they need to take your flesh and blood?"

Hanu studied the picture. It showed the DNA strands as he had seen them in his science books at school, but there were other strands as well, superimposed over the regular strand. It was illustrating evolved DNA. Hanu thought about the drugs he had been taking. He remembered the last time he and Akesh stood in line for their meds- the day that brought him here. 'What do you think about the new drugs? Tastes a little like blood...' He imagined an Ancient One putting blood into capsules with a dropper and shipping them off to the Flush. Akesh wasn't even phased by the medicines they were giving him. He must be the biggest threat against the Ancients. And the girls, too. These girls were taking their meds and still had enough fight to see through the lies.

"I wasn't even supposed to be here," he accidentally said out loud. But then he heard his own voice and looked around to see everyone looking at him, so he had to explain. "I'm not strong, or special or anything like that. I decided to stop taking my meds on a whim and they found out. I was breaking the rules, and that's the only reason I was even on that trip."

"Hanu, everything happens for a good reason," Ester said, trying to reassure him. And the other girls helped.

"If you weren't on that trip we would have never survived, Hanu. You're the one who introduced us to Harris," Vanessa said. Sadie gave him what was supposed to be a reassuring pat on the back, but he fell forward into the table.

"Ever think that you decided to stop taking your meds because you were strong enough to recognize the truth?" Paula asked gently. Then she gave him a second slap on the back. "Stop acting like a prepubescent dandelion. You made it this far for a reason, and apparently, you were integral to the mission."

But Hanu was already deflated, and his mind was going again. He thought about the state of the world and the people he loved. He thought about his mom. She was so happy the day she got her job as a geneticist. He was six years old. That night she kept saying, 'I'm a real scientist now!' And his sister. She was always so bubbly and happy. Maybe he'd be happier if he were like them, unaware of any of these realities. He wondered if his mom knew about the genetic experiments in the District of Operations. And he hoped they didn't find a way to stay on Earth for good this time.

"How do we survive this?" he asked. "This is so unfair- this life. We're so helpless. Aren't there other beings out there that want to help us? It can't just be us and them."

Paula turned to a page in the middle of the book, and passed it over to Ester.

"There is actually a faction of extra dimensional beings that are helpful. They tip the balance, if you will. But these beings respect the rules of non-interference. They cannot fight our entire battle for us because then humanity will never learn to stand on its own two feet, but they do lend help from time to time. They offer advice, and sometimes knowledge," she said.

"Well where are they? How do we get in contact with them?" Ester asked, sliding the book over for Vanessa to see.

"Humans are naturally capable of astral travel. We can enter a pretty wide range of dimensions that harmonize with our own vibrational frequency, temporarily of course. There, we are able to meet with these beings," Paula explained.

"Cool," said Sadie as she looked at the picture. "So how do we do this astral travel stuff?"

Sadie slid the book over to Hanu. There was an illustration of a different assortment of creatures. Some were insect-like and others looked more human except they were either taller or shorter and had varying colors of skin. There were a few that looked kind of like the Ancients, but Hanu could tell the distinctions. Two of the beings didn't even really have bodies, they were just orbs of light. Hanu recognized one that he'd seen before- with a brown, wrinkled little face and wispy whiskers protruding from underneath its long beard.

Chapter Seven

"You do it every night," Paula said. "It happens in your dreams."

Hanu's heart stopped beating altogether. He put his nose to the page, studying the features of the being. He looked at the inscription below the illustration: Galedeus, Nergal: Ambassador of the Intergalactic Council, 5th dimension.

"That's enough for today, gang," Paula said, pulling the book from under his nose and placing it on a desk underneath the staircase. "Let's eat."

Three days later someone arrived with a shipment of goods.

"It's time you guys put a little work in for the world class vacation you're getting here," Paula said as she doled out instructions. "Jars of food go in that pantry over there, Hanu. Stack them nice and tight, okay? Vanessa, if you will, change out the light bulbs in the growing room over there. My vegetables haven't been getting much attention lately. I've been waiting on these sun lights to come in for days. They might be dead. Ellie please stop eating the carrots."

Hanu was dragging the food over to the pantry. His body was very sore now and the heavy box didn't help. He didn't mind too much, though. He was happy to be of use. And once he was finished, he'd go and get the Tome and read some more. As of late he'd been reading up on interdimensional beings and astral travel to the fifth dimension. He had to read through a lot of material to glean what he really wanted, so it was tedious, but well worth it.

He got the box over to the pantry under the stairs but now he was struggling to get it open.

“Back up,” Paula said as she brought a knife down into the side of the box. Then she put the knife on the desk and went on to help Sadie store the dry goods.

After everyone was finished unpacking and breaking down the boxes Paula brought out a loaf of bread and cut it up.

“Okay guys, the vegetables didn’t die after all, so tomorrow we’ll eat some good stuff. Today we have to eat the last of the bread, though,” she said with a sour face. Survival bread, she called it. They had been eating it for the last day and a half, and apparently she didn’t like it very much because sometimes that’s all she had to eat. But Hanu loved it. It was ordinary buttered bread, sprinkled with cinnamon and sugar.

“Okay kiddoes, you’ll be leaving the day after tomorrow. That’s when the Bowl officially starts, and with all of the celebrations in town the Council will have too much on their hands to be worried about you guys. It’s a three day journey,” Paula explained.

Hanu was hardly listening though. He scarfed down his bread and thanked Paula before excusing himself. Then he grabbed the Tome off of the desk and found a spot on the floor to read. He opened to a small section toward the back of the book titled *Astral Travel*.

Chapter Eight

The Two Cities

Hanu had been looking forward to dreaming as of late, but he had a strange dream that night. He was wearing a maroon robe while standing in line for his meds when Akesh showed up and said he'd be in trouble for being out of dress code. Then he struggled as Akesh tried to pull the robe off, and then Ellie came out of the nurse's station talking about the escape plan to the Underground. As Hanu tried to hush Ellie a scout walked up and asked if he could scan them. Hanu tried to run for it, but the scout opened his mouth and sounded an alarm.

He awoke with a start, but he could still hear the siren. He looked around the room, disoriented. He didn't remember where he was, and someone was pulling him onto the floor.

"Come on, Hanu! People are in here," Ester yelled at him. He jumped off of the floor. He could see through the glass that a couple of masked people in black were moving around downstairs, and another was rummaging in a room across the way.

"The documents!" he screamed over the siren, and he threw the door open. He could see that Ellie was tied up on the ground downstairs and one of them was grabbing her by the hair. Ester grabbed Hanu by the arm and pulled him down the stairs.

"Vanessa's taking care of the documents, Hanu. We need to move," she said.

Hanu stumbled to the bottom of the stairs. Vanessa was banging on the glass of the data room door, and Paula was tied up near the escape tunnel. One of the intruders was doubled over on the ground now, and Sadie was wresting away from another, who had grabbed her from behind.

It wasn't real to Hanu. He just watched as Vanessa was screaming something over the noise. Ester was punching the blinking button in the box, and he was just standing there. He could tell that the women had been struggling. Junk was scattered about on the floor- papers, boxes and the knife from yesterday. Now Ellie was yelling something. He looked at her lips, trying to read what she was saying.

"Kill me! Hurry up!" she yelled, gesturing to the knife with her wide blue eyes.

He walked over to where the knife was. *Destroy the data, take the tunnel, and if they're caught, we have to kill them.*

He couldn't kill anyone though, not even to save thousands of people. But things weren't looking too good, and he had to help somehow. He moved without thinking, running over to where Ellie was. He jumped on top of the masked figure and thrust his elbow into his face on impact. They both fell down, nearly sliding into the water.

Ester ran to untie Ellie and Sadie was now sitting on top of the intruder she had been struggling with, punching relentlessly. Then the alarm abruptly stopped and the intruders raised their hands in surrender.

“That’s enough,” Paula said, unraveling the rope from around her legs. Sadie, whose arm was still raised, was the first to speak.

“Somebody better explain something to me real quick. Are we being raided or not?” She was breathing hard.

“We’re not,” Paula said, walking over to help the intruders off of the floor. The one who had been rummaging around in the rooms came to the bottom of the stairs, taking his mask off. His face was mostly hair, forming a wooly cloud around his chin and head, and he wore an assortment of bags and colorful stones on beaded rope around his neck.

“It was a test,” Ester guessed.

Sadie stood up, sweeping her hair out of her face.

“Yes, it was a test,” Paul said. “And a poorly designed one, I might add.” She helped the intruder to remove his mask, reveling that it was, in fact, a woman. She had long orange hair and kind eyes. Her soft face was beginning to swell on one side.

The others removed their masks as well, and Ellie crossed the room to help the man who had just served as Sadie’s punching bag.

"These people are ferries to the Underground. They will be taking you there tomorrow. They often help me to test the migrants who come through here," she explained. But Hanu cut her off.

"Test us for what, exactly?" He was angry to have been subjected to such a cruel trick.

"First, an artificial human would have done everything correctly when executing my plan. We were captured, and the orders were to kill us in that case. Congratulations, none of you are artificial. Second, I wanted to see that you would try your best to protect the Underground, and I wanted to make sure you weren't the type of people who would blindly follow directions- that you would carry out the task, but still maintain a sense of moral integrity. I'll admit, I thought our intruders could take a few hits from a couple of girls and a prepubescent dandelion if all went as planned, but I didn't expect this one-" and she pointed to Sadie. "-to be such a loose cannon."

"I thought we were in danger! You can't fault me for that," Sadie defended. Then Ellie, who looked like she would explode from trying to stay quiet this whole time, cut in.

"Well actually, Sadie, that was perfectly acceptable, you know…you decided you'd rather try to disable the enemy rather than offing us…thank you for that, by the way…but I guess I'm trying to say that…"

"Thank you Ellie, that was eloquently said," Pula said, cutting back in. "You followed your moral and rational compasses, albeit you have deadlier fists than I've seen in a while. We can't just let any old psychopath who would kill without batting an eye into the Underground."

Chapter Eight

But Vanessa was furious. "We could have murdered you!" she said, stomping her foot and crossing her arms. Tears were welling up in her eyes. "And that stupid button wasn't working and I was two seconds away from breaking that glass and throwing all the data into the water!"

"But you didn't, so stuff it," Paula retorted. "That's not a data room anyway, it's a storage closet."

Then Ellie was giggling nervously again. "I'm so sorry for tricking you guys! That was so hard to do with a straight face! You did an excellent job, though, really…Please forgive us," she said. "I've got to introduce our friends, Paula, if you don't mind."

Hanu winced at the man he had just elbowed in the face. He was feeling quite guilty as he watched blood trickle out of his nose.

"Everyone, this is Reginald and Anderson, from the City of Fire," she said, dramatically gesturing toward the man at the stairs and the man who was Sadie's last victim.

"Hi, just call me Reggie," said the man at the stairs.

The other man, Anderson, who was now holding a cold compress to his face, waved with his free hand.

"And you can call me Andy. No need to be so formal, Ellie," he said.

Andy's prominent, round eyes gave him the appearance of someone who was very knowing. His head, in contrast to Reggie's, had very little hair and he wore fingerless gloves on his hands.

"And these two are John and Moira, from the Underground," she said, pointing to each of them in turn. The man spoke first.

"Hey, everyone. I'm obviously John," he laughed good-naturedly, despite the fact that he'd just been dealt a pretty good blow to the face. The man was on the shorter side, and he had a long brown beard that made him look sagely.

"I'm Moira. Nice to meet you all," the woman said, waving timidly.

Hanu had been so terrified. He was relieved that it was just a drill, but the anxiety that he amassed just had to be released somehow. He laughed out loud.

"I'm so sorry I hit you," he said louder than he meant to. John waved the apology away, walking over to shake Hanu's hand.

"I'm not," Sadie said stubbornly as she side-eyed Andy. "Serves you right for tricking us. Plus, you need to learn to take a punch," she smiled wryly.

"Woah, woah, woah," Andy said, raising both a finger and his eyebrows. "I was allowing you to hit me because it was a test. But if you want a round two we can go for real. Paula will be the ref, won't you Paula?"

Andy was wearing the same competitive smile as Sadie now, and Paula was scoffing at the two. But before they could get going, Hanu interrupted.

"So are there two Underground cities?"

"Goodness, no," Moira said. "Globally, there have to be dozens, but on this continent there's the main city and then there are other smaller cities that serve as outposts. People there sort of specialize in different functions, but they all work together to protect the Underground.

“We’ve got plenty of time to talk about the Underground later,” Paula cut in. “Can we please clean up so that we can have some semblance of order here. Reginald, I don’t know what you were doing up there, but you better not had damaged any of my furniture.”

ஐஐஐஐஐஐஐஐ

Later on that night Hanu joined Vanessa and Moira at the table downstairs. Vanessa was laying across two chairs, gazing across the water at the pyramid. Paula was beeping messages through her box under the stairs and Reggie was setting up a fire pit.

“You don’t mind me building the fire this close to the water, do you, Paula?” he asked.

“Please do, Reginald. I haven’t forgotten how you almost took down the entire cave last month,” she said over her shoulder.

Reggie threw his head back in a booming cackle. “It was just a little bonfire, to lighten the mood,” he said.

Hanu thought that this is what having a family must be like. It had been so long since he was home, and it was just him and his mother for the most part. He never knew the feeling of aunts and uncles, cousins and siblings. Well, beside Kait, but all she could do was chew on things. He never had anyone to exchange jokes with, and he didn’t know how to produce witty comebacks. Maybe he’d learn if he went to the City of Fire with Reggie and Andy.

Moira picked up her guitar and started strumming as they watched Reggie build the fire.

"So how long have you guys been doing this? You know, taking people to the Underground?" Hanu asked.

"Me and Andy have been going at this for maybe four years now," Reggie said as he stacked bricks in a circle. "John's been doing it for about twenty years, and Moira- she's pretty new."

And the music stopped for a moment.

"Seven months," she said, and started playing again.

"We only take this trip once a month though. Other teams rotate in as well," Reggie continued.

"So you guys come from two different cities. Are we going to be going to separate places then?" Hanu asked.

"Well, representatives usually come from the City of Fire to check out the new people. That way everyone's on the same page. We keep track of our citizens, but nowhere near like what's going on with the Council up there," she explained.

"Sometimes we take people back to the City of Fire with us, though," Reggie said, fitting a rack onto the bricks now.

"Well what do people in the City of Fire do? And how do you decide who goes to the City of Fire and who goes to the Underground?" Hanu asked.

"Well the people who go to the Underground just want to live in peace, basically," Moira explained. "And it is peaceful. It's so different and free, Hanu. Some people want nothing more to do with life on the surface, so they leave everything behind and they're okay with it. One day the Ancients will have to leave, and we wait patiently until they do."

Hanu thought about everything he'd left behind. His mother, Kait, Akesh, Jeremiah, Titanya and the others at the Flush.

Vanessa suddenly laughed. "That's what I want to do, leave it all behind," she said. Hanu didn't realize she was listening.

Then Reggie cut in. "Other people can't just do that," he said as he lit the fire in the pit. "They can't just stand by and let these bastards have their way with our planet and our people. The ones who end up coming with us just have a fire in them. They do something about it. They can't help but fight the system."

"Which they do by acting as defense for the people in the Underground," Paula cut in, sitting down at the table now. "The people in the City of Fire are responsible for the delicious lemon drink that Toni provided you, and for disabling control systems of the Ancients so that others like you can escape their clutches. They also gather useful information and data. They help when and how they can to bring the control system down faster."

Moira was strumming a little softer now. "Ultimately the decision is yours. I'd think that a couple of kids like you can live a happy life in the Underground, though. Well, Sadie might choose the City of Fire. Her right hook would be dead useful, too," she said, laughing. Reggie laughed, too, as he threw the vegetables on the pit.

"So they were taking you guys in for override, huh?" she asked.

"Yeah, apparently so. The escorts told us that we were going in so the Ancients could help us, though. He said they wanted to do some research of some sort. But we figured it out when the scout told us we'd be getting an Easement Request," Hanu explained.

"Well that's usually what they do," Reggie said with gritted teeth. "They keep you alive just enough so that their geneticists can use your blood and cells, then when they're done with their experiments who knows what they do to you."

"Wow, that sounds like a doozy," Sadie said, coming down the stairs now.

"They must've felt real threatened after it started raining. They couldn't even wait until the Bowl to take you guys in!" Moira said.

"Well I'm sure the Council didn't want their fun spoiled by having to off a couple of kids during half time," Sadie said, smirking.

"Well that's when they kill the most people," Moira said. "It's sickening. When the whole world is out celebrating they use the distraction. Ever notice Council invites all these special people into the District of Operations during the Bowl? Then there's always a reason to detain one group or another. You never hear anything else about it afterward."

"But the people they detain are dangerous," Hanu said.

"And just how do you know that?" Reggie asked, looking at Hanu with a raised brow.

"Well, everyone knows it. It's people like the Dissenters that they take. The Dissenters are dangerous- they kill people," he said.

"Hey, you hear that, Andy? The Dissenters kill people!" Reggie shouted up the stairs.

"And you know that because the TV told you, right?" he continued, looking back at Hanu.

"Well, yeah," Hanu said, feeling a little silly now. He knew where this was going now, and he was grateful for Paula speaking up for him.

"Give the kid a break, Reginald," she said.

"Oh, I'm just having some fun, I'm sorry," he said. "And just so you know, they would label anyone as a threat to public safety to justify killing them, you included. There is no such group as the Dissenters."

"He's right," Moira added darkly. "And then they're taking in those fourteen kids from the Flush this year. I bet you anything they'll say the kids rioted and that they had no choice but to detain them."

"Are they going to kill them?" he asked a little more forcefully than he intended. Moira stopped playing the guitar, slowly shaking her head.

"I'm so sorry. You have friends there, don't you? I should have been more sensitive," she was saying, but Hanu didn't hear her. His thoughts were going again. The Council was eliminating everyone who was a threat to the system. Akesh would be going to the District, and he was the biggest threat Hanu could think of. None of the medicines they gave him worked. He was immune. He wondered if they would use his DNA to figure out how to stop other kids in the future from building an immunity.

“So do they always kill them?” he asked again, a little calmer this time.

Moira looked at the others nervously. She wasn’t sure how much more she should say. But she didn’t have to say anything else because Paula answered the question for her.

“Yes. That is the design of the plan. The Council does not care about the Bowl, or the special guests they have invited in to watch it. They only care about ensnaring their latest victims. This is a truth that you have to understand, and it won’t even be the ugliest truth you’ll hear in your days. I’m sorry, kiddos. I hope you don’t have friends in that parade.”

Vanessa looked pained, and Sadie quietly fumed.

“Seriously?” Hanu asked. He was no longer himself. His hands were hot and shaking, and it was getting harder to breathe. He stood up. “You guys knew about this all along, and you were just going to let it happen?

“There isn’t much we can do, Hanu,” Vanessa said quietly.

“What do you mean? We can warn them! We can help them escape! We can make the Convoy blow up like last time!” Hanu stood up, looking around wildly now. He knew that what he was saying couldn’t be done so easily, but he felt that it *could* be done.

“We’re so powerful and all of that and we can’t even help our friends? We didn’t ask to be different. We didn’t ask to go to the Flush. Why do we have to suffer like this?” he went on.

"Hanu, shut your mouth!" Sadie said, quelling his outburst. "You think it's easy for them? To see everything for what it is and not have enough power to stop it? I'm sure that if they could, they would do something about it. But they have to be smart, Hanu. They have to protect the Underground."

Hanu threw himself back into his seat, seething. He would have figured Sadie would be the one to agree with him on this one.

"Trust me, Hanu. If we could save every last person up there, we would," Reggie said. "I've had friends die at the hands of the Council, too."

Sadie was right. They couldn't risk their safety, and the safety of the Underground for a couple of people. But he hadn't gone to the Underground and he didn't know all of those people. He knew Akesh, and Akesh was a good person. Hanu got up and went to his room.

"I'm going to bed," he said over his shoulder.

Chapter Nine

In the District

Hanu got out of bed somewhere on the other side of the midnight hour. He had been going back and forth in his mind, trying to find reason enough to turn from everything and never look back. He couldn't quite do that now. And he still really didn't see himself just ferrying people to the Underground like Paula and the others. That was still too passive. He thought about what Reggie said about the people from the City of Fire- that they had a fire burning within them, that they couldn't help but fight the system. Hanu didn't think Reggie knew what he was talking about. Hanu had a real fire in his gut, and it wouldn't allow him to just sit back and laugh it up while people were out there dying.

That's why he was running away. Hanu planned it all out while everyone else was downstairs for dinner. Ester had been in bed for the last couple hours, snoring gently, but he had to wait until Paula fell asleep. After everyone else had climbed the stairs for bed, she stayed up securing the tunnels and enabling the alarms. Then she sat at her desk at the bottom of the stairs, sending her messages. Hanu could hear her tapping the little lever and then minutes later, receiving a message back in little beeps. She spent an hour or so doing this while Hanu impatiently waited.

Chapter Nine

Now she was retired to her room and enough time had passed for her to have fallen asleep, so Hanu slipped out of his bed and down the stairs. First he opened the pantry. He took four jars of peaches and a loaf of bread, and put it in the bag that Harris had sent them with. He would eat one jar on the way to the Bathtub Resort, and stash the rest in the tunnel for the return journey. If all goes as planned he would need the extra food for Akesh, and anyone else he could save along the way.

Then Hanu found the knife in the desk drawer. He might need it as a tool, or perhaps to defend himself with. He stashed it in his back pocket, along with the flashlight he'd been using to read the Tome late at night. He snuck to the pool and bottled some water, then drank a few handfuls. He knew he would need to be hydrated for the walk ahead.

Now the tricky part. Hanu had seen Paula disengage the alarm on a couple occasions, but he never had reason to pay real attention. He was pretty certain he could do it, though. The day they got their food and supplies delivered, he remembered looking at the pad and thinking the passcode was too easy. She had just gone up one side of the pad and down the other. Then she hit the green button, which said 'send'.

Hanu opened the cover of the box and traced the pattern to jog his memory. It looked about right, so he hit the first button: #. The beep echoed off the quiet walls. He didn't think about the sound it would make. But everyone was asleep, and the glass doors should serve as a buffer against the sound. He pressed the next button: 9. Then he paused. "Why does this code have to be so *long*?" he agonized.

Still, nobody stirred, so he pressed the succession of keys as quickly as he could: 6 3 1 4 7 *, send.

Click.

He did it. The doors were unlocked now. But he didn't want to leave it unlocked all night, so he ran over and propped it open with a rock. Then he grabbed his bag and reengaged the alarm. Hanu was free now. He strolled through the door.

And straight into someone.

"Aaaagh!" he screamed uncontrollably, clutching for the knife in his back pocket. It fell to the ground with a loud clank, so he abandoned it and tried to pull the door shut behind him. At least everyone else would have a fighting chance to escape.

Whoever it was started laughing hysterically. Hanu recognized it; a deep cackle.

"Why would you do that to me, Reggie?" he asked indignantly.

"Well, dang," he said, doubled over now. "I didn't know you would scream like that!"

Now Reggie was gasping for air and slapping his knee.

"Shhh! You're going to wake everyone up," Hanu said.

"No, sir. You did that," Reggie said, laughing still. "I think the Council might even know where we are now."

Hanu's heart was still racing. He looked through the cracked door to see if anyone had been awakened by the debacle. Ester was coming down the stairs now.

"See what you did?" he hissed. "Ester's awake now. Why are you even here? Don't you know you're being creepy?"

"Look, Hanu, we're not going to let you go into the District all by yourself. That's suicide," he said, serious now.

"You knew I would run away?" Hanu asked. "How?"

"Everyone knew you were going to do something stupid, Hanu, we all saw it on your face," he said. "Plus, everyone pulls the 'I'm going to bed' routine. This isn't our first time around the block. We knew you were up there plotting."

"So does this mean you're not going to stop me? Are you coming with me then?" he asked hopefully.

"Of course, man. Andy's coming, too- he's getting his bag ready now," Reggie said, ushering him back into the cave. "We're from the City of Fire. We're not gonna let you outburn us."

Ester met them at the door. "Hanu it's important that you listen," she started.

"Ester I'm going, and nothing you're going to say will stop me. Akesh will be going to the district tomorrow and Jeremiah might be there, too."

"Which is why I'm not going to stop you," she said. "You are special and strong, Hanu. You were brave enough to try to run away and do it all on your own."

Hanu didn't know what to say. His face was starting to burn and he was suddenly aware of Reggie and Andy grinning at each other. He nodded his head.

“Listen,” she said. “When the Convoy crashed, I checked out the navigation route. They were taking us to some sort of holding facility- the furthest building the southwest in the district. The only entrance is from the east. You have to go through what looks like a tunnel system that wraps around the main building. You’ll save yourself some time if you can breech that tunnel and go straight to the facility.”

“Wait, why were you worried about the navigation route?” Hanu asked. “I mean, don’t get me wrong, I’m grateful you had that information, but why weren’t you just worried about surviving like the rest of us?”

“Well, I figured the information was there for the taking, why not, huh? It wouldn’t hurt to know where they were taking us,” she said.

“We could use someone like you on the team, Ester,” Andy said, amazed.

“Yeah, you wanna tag along?” Reggie asked.

“Oh, no. I’m not that brave,” Ester said, laughing.

“Look, we need to get out of here before Paula wakes up,” Reggie said, glancing nervously up the stairs. Andy put on his backpack and they headed toward the door.

“Hey, Ester,” Hanu said, turning back.

“Yeah, Hanu?”

He wasn’t sure if he wanted to know the answer, but he still couldn’t help but ask. “Will we be okay?”

Chapter Nine

Ester seemed to be debating if she should answer him. She looked at Andy and Reggie, then back to Hanu. "You will," she finally said.

He wasn't sure if she was just saying it to keep his spirits up or if she actually believed they'd be okay. She smiled at Hanu, and he gave her a quick nod before walking out of the door

The men moved swiftly through the damp tunnel. Andy insisted on a steady jog the whole way because they'd be taking a longer route, but Hanu was doing more of a bungling shuffle. He ignored the pain in his side, though, because he knew that lives were on the line, and he shuffled on.

Hanu remembered the one year his mom took him to the Bowl. He was only five, but he remembered that day well. He wasn't quite as interested in the actual game as he was just participating in the fun. Mom let him wear maroon glitter lashes, just like hers, to support her team. They packed into the streets early that morning, and had to shuffle sideways to get a good spot for the parade. He remembered sitting on her shoulders and waving as the procession came down the street.

There were giant animated floats and decorated people dancing and waving at them. That was the first time he saw an Ancient in real life. The pale being was so big you could fit two or three humans into it. It was terrifying. And all the stories he heard about the might and power of the saviors were real in that moment. These creatures were real. Hanu also remembered the band of Convoys at that parade. He wasn't very interested in them because they were so scarcely decorated. They just sported simple team flags. It was anticlimactic in comparison.

He fell asleep halfway through the game and didn't wake until they were already home. He remembered being upset when he shot up, ready to scream at the top of his lungs, only to find his mom sitting in the living room with the news anchors. They were telling her that people had tried to assassinate one of the Ancients.

'The assailants have been detained and Agrigore will make a full recovery. Unfortunately, after lack of cooperation they were sentenced to override', she told mom with a reassuring smile. Hanu wondered if it was the people in that Convoy that were detained that day, but he already knew the answer. He was so embarrassed now, for being happy about it when he heard the news.

"Yeah, you don't mess with the Gods!" he yelled with a tiny raised fist.

He was such a stupid kid for being happy about other peoples' sentence to override.

Almost four hours later they stopped jogging. Hanu had run through the pain in his side and caught a second wind, so he was reluctant to stop, but a new pain in his stomach insisted he did.

"So what exactly was your plan, man?" Andy asked, pulling the loaf of bread apart.

"Well, I was gonna turn myself in, then bust us all out," Hanu said through a mouthful of bread.

Chapter Nine

"You were going to turn yourself in? So you were just going to walk up to the District doors and ring the bell?" he asked incredulously.

"Well, more like crash the parade," Hanu said, smirking. "I thought about flipping the Convoy somehow, but I hadn't figured out all the details just yet."

"This kid's insane," Andy said to Reggie, laughing. Hanu took it as a compliment.

"Sounds like someone I know at that age," Reggie said. "You got some guts, man, but that's not the best position to put yourself in."

"So what do you suggest we do?" Hanu asked.

"Oh, I've got a few tricks in my bag. I think we can cook up a good plan," Andy said, smiling wickedly.

❧❧❧❧❧❧❧❧

The tunnel that they took led them right into a sewer in the Business District. It was convenient, too, that a large Ferris wheel was being constructed nearby, because they were able to emerge from the manhole unnoticed. From there, it was a short walk to the District wall.

He had never seen it this close before. The wall was so tall he got dizzy trying to see the top of it. It felt like he would fall into it if he wasn't careful enough. Hanu decided he'd just look straight ahead. Though the wall was just brick and mortar, it scared him. They were in way over their heads. How could three people break into such a place unnoticed?

Fortunately, though, the parade was over and people were now meandering through the surrounding court. The swarm of oddly dressed people and decorated tents around the fortress provided ideal cover for their movements. These festivities would continue for at least three more hours until the games started, so they had time to form a plan. They rested briefly under a canopy with a couple of friendly college students who had travelled from University. They kept screaming wildly and occasionally trying to shove drinks into their hands, but other than that the trio was able to plan in peace.

"We're going to see how good of an actor you are today, Han," Reggie said as he handed Hanu a necklace with a bulky charm on it.

"Am I going to pretend to be you today, then?" Hanu asked facetiously.

Maybe it was because he was finally out in the open sunlight and about to save his friend or, more likely, because of the lack of sleep and physical exhaustion, but Hanu was feeling quite bold. He even considered having a beer, but he knew he'd need all of his mental faculties in order to carry out his task.

"You've got jokes. I like that," Reggie said. Andy was slapping Reggie on the back, laughing at him. "Seriously, though. We've been working on this piece of technology for the last two years. It's a holographic cloak."

"So it'll hide us?" Hanu asked, turning it over in his hands.

"Even better- it'll make you look like scout. It cloaks your body in a hologram," Reggie said.

Chapter Nine

"No way!"

Andy, nodding his head proudly, put one around his own neck and smoothed his hand over the charm.

"So I'll have to act like a scout, huh?" Hanu asked. He hadn't interacted with very many scouts, so he wasn't really sure how they acted.

"It'll be fine. Just act like an uptight know-it-all and only speak when you're spoken to," Andy said.

"Okay, act like a scout. Then what?"

"Then we stroll through the front door and bust your friends out," Reggie said.

❧❧❧❧❧❧❧

But strolling through the front door seemed more of a challenge than they thought. Hanu thought maybe someone would be working the front gate and would simply let them in, but apparently they were required scan their palms for entry. Reggie suggested that they find a real scout and cut its arm off, but they eventually agreed that it would cause too much unnecessary attention. Plus, it was just crazy.

So they decided to pace the entrance and wait for a real scout to enter. Then they'd follow behind. Hanu tried to look the part. He straightened himself as much as he could as he strode through the streets. Occasionally someone would ask him for directions to a nearby bathroom or if the public shuttles would be running on alternative schedules. He didn't know the answer to either of those questions, so he did the best he could to bluff. Andy was able to acquire a yellow Suns bag from a street vendor to better blend with the Bowl festivities.

Their patience was rewarded shortly after kickoff. A single scout entered the gate, and they quietly followed. It was just as Ester said- a large tunnel. Once inside, they slowed, allowing the real scout to continue without them. He climbed a set of stairs in the distance where the tunnel turned off to the right. That must be where the entrance to the main building is, Hanu thought. He ran his hand across the smooth surface of the tunnel, looking for a weak spot. It was metal, just like the street. There was no way to breech it.

“Well, we have no other choice,” Reggie said. “Let’s go in and find a way to the holding facility from there.”

They walked through the tunnel, as the real scout had, and climbed the stairs. They found that it led to a palace. It was grander than Hanu could have imagined, with high vaulted ceilings and unusually tall doors. The walls were decked with mirrors and elegant portraits, and velvety curtains covered floor-to-ceiling windows. There was a majestic staircase winding up to the second floor. Its steps weren’t built for humans. It was built for the giants that dwelled there. There was a large spread of various food and drinks set up along one wall, which was unattended now because everyone was watching the game.

Hanu walked along the wall, looking through the windows. He could see a well landscaped lawn and in the distance, only a couple hundred yards, away was a shiny building.

Chapter Nine

"Hey guys, could that be it?" he asked. Reggie and Andy were crossing the room now to have a look. He knew it was them, but couldn't help but be alarmed as he turned around and saw them approaching.

"No that building is straight to the south," Reggie said, gauging the sun. "But if we get there, all we'd have to do is look to the west, right?

"Let's find a way out," Andy said.

They had no choice but to explore a corridor off of the main room. There were no other doors in the main room beside the one they arrived through. They occasionally passed another scout or a guest, or member of administration. Andy and Reggie's matching faces were both placid and charming. Hanu knew he was wearing too much angst to be playing his role well. He kept looking at his feet to make sure the cloak hadn't come undone. That would be the last thing they needed right now.

"Hanu look down here," Reggie said, pointing to a door at the bottom of a short flight of stairs. It looked like it could be a way out to the grounds. Hanu went for it. And the door opened to a lush green lawn.

"You don't get grass like this just anywhere nowadays!" Andy said playfully.

"That's top notch grass right there," Reggie agreed blithely.

"Shhh," Hanu warned. Though he didn't have much experience with them, he was certain that scouts didn't go around analyzing the quality of grass.

"Nobody's around, Hanu, lighten up," Andy said.

"Just come on, guys, the building's this way."

The trio walked toward the building to the south, and it would have been uneventful had they not been stopped by an Ancient One, of all people. They saw the figure off to the right, walking up a cobbled path to the main palace like a giant animated marble statue. Before they could hide, it spotted them and cut through the grass to meet them. All they could do was straighten their faces and move forward to greet it. Hanu didn't have the same feeling about the Ancients as he once had. Its grandeur evoked fear now, instead of awe, and he struggled to keep his face from showing it as the creature approached.

"What purpose do you serve here?" It spoke in a low wispy voice. Hanu could feel something strange happening to his body. He was feeling heavy, weighted to the Earth. Was this the power of an Ancient One?

"Well that is the existential question that all intelligent life ponders, but a definite conclusion is effectively unattainable," Andy said, much to everyone else's horror.

"But the purpose we specifically serve here on the grounds," Reggie said, eyeing Andy as angrily as he could while pretending to be a scout, "-is to ensure security of the perimeter."

"No orders were given for such security," the creature said, looking down on them inscrutably.

"This is the night of the Bowl party, and intel has been received suggesting that Dissenters may attempt to breech the wall. With current arrangements, it is agreed to err on the side of caution," Reggie said with a straight face.

Chapter Nine

"And for this measure, you are patrolling in a triad," the Ancient said. Hanu wasn't sure if he was asking or simply observing. He never thought about it before, but he's never seen scouts travel in a group before- only in pairs or alone.

"Temporarily," Andy said, catching on, too. "Once the perimeter is secured we will resume basic patrol. So far we have only collected inconsequential memorabilia misplaced by guests."

Andy was referring to his Suns bag that the Ancient was eyeing now.

"Very well," it said, almost in a whisper, as it walked away.

"What was that, you idiot?" Reggie asked Andy in an outrage once the Ancient was out of earshot.

"I think that's exactly what a scout would have said, Reg. I think you're overreacting," he defended

Hanu didn't care to join in on the quarrel. He stood, watching it walk away, and wondering what the strange feeling was. He was devoid, cold. He was just relieved that they managed to survive the encounter despite his inability to help the situation.

The building they were headed for was quite close now, and Hanu could see that it was some sort of greenhouse. The sun was reflecting off of its glassy walls. Off to the right, further down the path that the Ancient had come from, Hanu could see what might have been the tunnel over the treetops.

"Hey, guys, let's follow that path. I bet you it leads us to the holding facility," he suggested.

"Let's move it," Reggie said, moving a little faster now. "And once we get there we'll have to split up. I don't want to attract much more attention."

"Yeah, that may be a good idea. We might be able to use it to our advantage, too," Andy said.

"I'll go," Reggie said, looking off into the distance. "I know what you're thinking, give me the dummies."

"What are dummies?"

"They're decoys," Andy said, digging in his bag now. "Really, they're experiments gone wrong, but we figured they'd make good distractions."

Andy gave Reggie a handful of small black spheres, which he placed in his pocket.

"They're roving holograms. Tried to use them as spies, but we just couldn't figure out how to control them well enough remotely. They're not very convincing when you talk to them, but they do run fast over flat surfaces," Reggie explained. "I'm going to make a scene while you guys escape. Once you're outside of the wall just blend with the crowd, then make your way to the Ferris wheel. Just make sure everyone understands the plan before you go, okay?"

Hanu was putting the plan in his mind-*escape, blend, Ferris wheel*. He could see now what should have been the building. It had no sign, but he could see that it was the furthest building to the southwest, and it was the last stop on the tunnel system. This had to be the place.

The building had sliding glass doors, and looked rather welcoming for a torturous holding place for prisoners of genetic experimentation. Whether a code or a scan was needed, they were unsure. But it didn't matter because just as they approached, another scout was exiting through the doors and they slid right in.

They found themselves in a spacious lobby.

"Great, are you here to help prepare the rooms for our guests?" the receptionist asked, getting up to meet them at the door. Her high heeled steps echoed off the walls.

Hanu was afraid that they had come to the wrong place. This seemed like a hotel more than a laboratory. There were no test tubes or Bunsen burners filled with bubbling colorful liquids- no equipment of any sort- and no test subjects. They didn't come here to change bedsheets- they came to rescue his friends. Reggie and Andy were a little apprehensive, too, but they kept their heads.

"Yes, we are. Could you tell us if there are any specifics regarding these preparations?" Andy said coolly to the woman.

"You know what, I'll walk you up," she said, leading them to the elevators. "It's a pretty large party. This group is genetically resistant to treatment, but they seem docile enough. Innocent little bunch… But you never know how they'll respond to stress, so you are to prepare electromagnetic fields in each room. Also, put a buzz on their doors. We can't afford a repeat of last week. Those twins caused quite an uproar in the hall."

Hanu's heart skipped a beat. The twins were here. Are they still alive? The woman was pushing the second floor button in the enormous elevator.

"And try to get one to a room this time. I'm not sure how many rooms are available, but we need at least fourteen. I know sometimes you just have to make do, but this group will be here for quite some time," she went on. "Frankly, the population is mutating too rapidly now, so we're going to try to get ahead of the curve with this one."

The scouts followed, listening, as she stepped off the elevator. Hanu tried to keep a vacant face as she went on talking about the operation with such nonchalance. He wanted to yell at her, to hit her, to knock some sense into her. Doesn't she care that they're taking over their world? Doesn't she want to be free? But he knew that reacting now would jeopardize their mission, and their mission was really the only thing he could control right now.

They walked down a wide hallway now. Hanu could see into the rooms, which were closed off only by a thin sheet of glass. This was more like the nightmare he imagined- beds fitted with metal cuffs, coolers stocked with vials of blood, beeping machines and tanks inhabited by tiny fetuses.

The sight was enough to fortify his resolve. Whatever regret he felt from running away from Deprogramming- for leaving the girls and jeopardizing his own safety- was gone now. He knew that Akesh and the others would be here soon, and this was no place for his friends. They reached a large chamber at the end of the hall, where two other people joined them. These men must have been nurses or assistants of some sort, because they had been bustling around finishing paperwork and cleaning up. They wore black jumpsuits similar to the ones the staff at The Flush wore.

"Great, you're here," one of them said. "We're just wrapping up for the night. Everything's finished on our end, and the guests will be arriving soon."

"Wonderful," the secretary said.

The other assistant closed the computers down. "Well let's get outta here!" he said, talking to his companion. "We're going to the party, Amy. Wanna come?"

"Alright, then. I'll leave it to you," Amy said to them as they walked out of the chamber. "Oh yeah, if you need anything, Delores will be in the downstairs lobby."

Reggie crossed the room and watched them get onto the elevator while Andy rushed through the double doors on the other side of the room. Hanu looked behind the desk, hoping to find some sort of useful information. He tried to pull up the computer screen, but it wouldn't budge. It must've required a scan. He looked over the various knobs and instruments along the wall.

"Guys, get down here," Andy said from the hall. They rushed through the doors after him and saw that he was at the end of a long hallway with small cells lining either wall. Hanu could see people in the rooms through mesh doors. Some were human and others weren't. Hanu recognized the insectoid features and bulbous bald heads of some of the races he'd studied in the Tome of the Earth. Some of them were just children. They couldn't have been older than six or seven. They sat in corners, hugging their knees or stood with their faces in the mesh, silently watching.

Hanu was sick. How could they save all these people? And even if they released them, were these feeble beings capable of running for their lives? Or would they all be captured again? He didn't see Tui or La, but he tried not to think about that right now. He didn't want to walk any further. He couldn't stand to see any more, but Andy was beckoning for them to hurry.

"It looks like this is the control system for the doors," he said, playing with knobs on a console. "It seems simple enough. You can open cell doors one at a time with these, but I'm not sure what those do."

Reggie turned one of the knobs. The mesh doors crackled loudly and one of the prisoners jumped back with a squeal.

"Electrical current. Must be the buzz Amy was talking about," Reggie said, turning the knob back down.

"And the electromagnetic field?" Andy said, playing with the other knobs.

"We need to help them," Hanu said. His voice was being choked out by a lump in his throat. He knew that they wouldn't agree to it, but how could Hanu save a few and leave the rest. How could he determine that some were worth saving and others weren't?

"Hanu, I know you want to save everyone, but I don't think that's possible. Some of these people are so far gone, I don't think it would be worth it," Reggie said, looking at a man in a nearby cell. He was staring at them, or perhaps, staring through them with vacant eyes. Hanu didn't argue it. He knew Reggie was probably right.

Chapter Nine

"Look, when your friends come in, tell them to stick close behind you when the doors open again," Reggie said. "I'm going to excuse myself after they arrive and then I'm going to give you fifteen minutes before I make the diversion. Once that happens, Andy is going to release all of the doors and lead you downstairs. Whoever can keep up will come with us."

"Then what?" Hanu asked.

"Then we escape through the hole in the wall," Andy said. He pulled two metal cylinders from his bag and attached them together.

"What hole?"

"The one I'm gonna blast through it," he said, handing Reggie the metal tube. "The elevator thing might be an issue, though. I didn't expect it to be on the second floor, and someone will be in the lobby."

"Got any flash bangers?" Reggie asked.

"No, but I have smoke bombs- Oh I see. I'll use those," he said.

There were nineteen vacant cells total. They were nothing more than small metal rooms. They smelled of various bodily fluids and something else- something Hanu recognized but couldn't quite put his fingers on. They cleaned them out with antiseptic soap they found in a closet and put fresh mats on the floors of the ones that would soon be inhabited. Shortly after they were finished they could hear struggling in the hallway.

Walking up and down the hallway full of prisoners had stressed Hanu to the point of being sick, and he was relieved in knowing that they would soon be able to free everyone. He wiped the sweat from his face a relaxed into a scout's composure just in time for a member of the council to emerge through the chamber doors. He wasn't anyone Hanu recognized, but the man was wearing a red tunic and brow band, as the other council members did.

"Oh, I wasn't aware we'd have extra hands," he said, brushing his disheveled hair back into place. "Help us bring them in."

He held the door open for Hanu to see a girl with a sack over her head on the floor, kicking wildly as two scouts tried to subdue her. Her hands were bound behind her. She landed a blow on one's face as he tried to pick her up from her shoulders.

"You're not taking me alive!" she yelled. "I knew this stupid trip wasn't right. You're trying to trick us!"

The others, whose hands were also bound, were allowing themselves to be ushered down the hall. They wore blindfolds, so scouts were walking alongside them, guiding them into the chamber.

"That's right," the councilman said to the prisoners in a very sweet voice over the girl's screaming. "With your cooperation this will be a very rewarding experience. Thank you for ignoring our confused friend here."

Andy and Reggie emerged from the back and immediately began helping the scouts secure the prisoners in their cells. Hanu couldn't tell who was who anymore until one of them gestured for him to grab someone and get moving. Hanu looked through the crowd, trying to find Akesh. He recognized some of them- Lisa, Mark and Sylvia, from his unit. Then there was Trent- one of Mr. Carlisle's other patients. He was starting to worry that he wasn't there, but then he saw them filing through the door. Akesh was curiously tugging at his blind and Jeremiah was close behind him. Hanu rushed over, relieved to have finally spotted them, and grabbed them by the elbows.

"This way to your suite, gentlemen," he said as he ushered them into the back hallway. As he bent to put Akesh in a sitting position in his cell, he whispered in his ear.

"Akesh, it's me, Hanu. Me and a couple friends are disguised as scouts. These people are going to kill you, but we're going to escape. Please don't make a sound. When the doors open again follow close behind us, okay?"

He hoped Akesh would believe him and keep quiet about it. He left his friend sitting in the cell, cocking his head curiously. Then Jeremiah allowed himself to be guided to a separate cell, where Hanu repeated himself.

"Okay," Jeremiah said, simply. He sat on his own in the middle of the room, aloof. Hanu wondered if he, like Ester, knew what would happen next.

Then Hanu was whisked to the front room to help with the screaming girl, who was now knocking things off the desk. Everyone else had tried to no avail, and most of the other scouts left, having completed their task of escorting them into the facility. She had just gotten her hands free, and was grabbing for the sack over her face. Hanu took advantage of her busy hands and grabbed her from behind just as she pulled it off- it was Titanya.

Hanu was a little nervous now. He never had the courage to talk to her and now he was in a full on hug with her. She clawed at him and all he could do was hold her tighter. He laughed at himself for being so awkward. Well, he could never start a conversation with her but at least today he would be able to set her free. Hanu looked around. The councilman was talking to three scouts. One of them was behind the desk now, typing something into the computer while the others looked on.

"I told you to always smile," he said in her ear, hoping it would shock her enough to listen. But it backfired on him.

"What is that supposed to mean, you weirdo?" she asked indignantly.

"Shhh, it's Hanu from the Flush," he whispered urgently, eyeing the desk. "I'm disguised as a scout. Don't worry, we're busting you out of here. But they're going to kill us if they catch us."

Either Andy or Reggie was turned around now, tight lipped, and gesturing toward the back hallway meaningfully. Titanya looked at him for a second, then conceded.

She allowed Hanu to take her to the back and lock her in one of the rooms.

"The next time these doors open, run. Follow me and the other scout downstairs. We're leaving soon," he reassured her.

When Hanu returned to the front desk the councilman was leaving. "I'm going to report to Agrigore now," he said. "Expect a call soon. I suspect he'll want to take that wild one downstairs with those troublesome twins." Then he took one last glance down the hallway and left.

Hanu couldn't be happier to have heard that. Everything was going as planned and even the twins were alive! He could imagine it- in just a few hours they'd all be back at Deprogramming. They just had to get rid of the last scout, but Andy was already on it.

"I believe the two of you should take a final patrol, to ensure security on the grounds. The Bowl will be nearly over by now," he said.

"That is not necessary. The remaining guests are secured in the media center and once the game is over they will be escorted back to the estate by Tameus, Jinora and Agrigore. The only threat we face has just been secured here."

Apparently that one was the real scout.

"I shall report back to the media center, then, and see if I can be of assistance," Reggie said, raising his brows behind the scouts back. The he slipped through the door and strode down the hall without skipping a beat.

Their time was running now: 15 minutes.

The scout walked over to the phone system and engaged it. "Upon orders, we will make a group effort to transport the miscreant downstairs. It will take two of us to hold her down while the third puts on the cuffs," he said.

That may be a good opportunity to see where the twins were being kept, Hanu thought. Maybe the call would come soon, and they would get downstairs and back in enough time for the diversion to start. But he didn't want Titanya to think he had betrayed her. He said that the next time the doors opened, that she would be free. What if she called him out on it? Would the other scout just brush it off as her being a delusional mental patient? And anyway, it would be difficult to break prisoners free from multiple floors once the diversion started. Hanu needed to talk to Andy, but the scout left very little room for a private conversation. He sat behind the desk, staring amiably into space.

Time was closing in on them, and after several attempts to send the scout elsewhere, Andy began picking up blunt objects from behind the desk and gauging whether or not he could hit the scout hard enough with it to knock him out. But it was too late.

Boom.

The scout stood up. “A single blast, a quarter of a mile to the north,” he judged.

“Respond to the emergency and report back. We’ll secure the guest in a downstairs room upon your return,” Andy said.

“Affirmative.”

The two watched the scout move down the hallway. He ran swiftly, and disappeared into the elevator in no time. Then Hanu turned to Andy.

“I have to save those twins downstairs,” he said.

“Hanu we can’t save everyone. That’s too dangerous. We don’t know the layout downstairs and we’re on borrowed time now. We need to be out of these walls in five minutes,” Andy said, rushing down the back hallway.

"Please," Hanu said. "Whatever they're doing to them down there, it has to be worse than this. Plus, if it weren't for those twins I wouldn't be free right now!"

And it was true. Hanu suspected that they were the ones who somehow caused the Convoy to flip in the first place. If anybody had manifesting power, it was them.

"What if you get caught? Is it worth it?" Andy asked, stopping at the console.

"It is," Hanu said looking Andy in the eyes. "Just make sure my friends make it to Deprogramming. I can find my own way back."

"Okay." And Andy brought his hands down on all of the buttons at once, opening the cells. "If you can keep up, follow me!" he yelled, running down the hall.

Hanu followed closely behind as everyone rushed out of their cells. Some of the beings seemed to just vanish into thin air, which Hanu thought was curious. Why hadn't they done that in the first place?

Seconds later they were crammed into the elevator. Hanu was squished up against a little boy he didn't recognize. He craned his neck to see if everyone he had come for made it. Akesh, Jeremiah, and Titanya- they were all amongst the group. When the bell rang on the first floor Andy rolled a handful of smoke bombs into the lobby. Delores screamed.

"Don't breathe it in," he yelled and he ran through the smoke to the doors. Hanu broke off from the group, running through the double doors on the opposite side of the lobby. This hallway was similar to the one upstairs. There were the same rooms and equipment behind thin glass walls, but toward the end of this hall there were several wooden doors and another hall cutting to the right. It was at the end of this hall that he found them: several prisoners all in one metal room.

They were barely alive, braced to the wall by shackles on their wrists. Hanu found the console and turned off the buzz, then threw the doors open. He grabbed one of the twins and shook his face.

“Hey, wake up. It’s Hanu.”

He couldn’t be roused. The boy’s lips were dried and bloody, and there was a deep purple bruise on his forehead. Hanu tried the other twin.

“Get up! We need to get out of here,” he yelled in the boy’s face. He grabbed at the shackles, looking to see if they required a key. They were smooth. The twin was moving his lips. He was whispering something. Hanu leaned in and put his ear to his mouth.

“I can’t feel my arms…”

Hanu ran back to the console. There must be a way to release the cuffs from the console, he thought. It looked just like the one from upstairs. Hanu toyed with the various buttons and knobs. He knew there wasn’t much time left and he wasn’t sure if he could drag the both of them through the building, let alone to the Ferris wheel. But he had come this far already, and luck had been on his side. He just had to find a way out through the back. Then they’d be closer to the wall, and the hole that Andy would blast through it.

Chapter Nine

Maybe once they were outside the twins would realize how close they were to freedom and snap out of it. He found the set of buttons that released the shackles. One by one the prisoners fell to the floor with agonized groans, too weak to catch themselves.

"What did they do to you?" he asked rhetorically as he propped one of the twins against the wall. Then he tried to wake the other.

"We're free. All you have to do is walk through those doors with me," he urged helplessly. "Please, your life depends on it. Let's go."

Grief was washing over him now as he backed away from the boys. There was nothing he could do. It was too late.

Boom.

Andy blasted the hole in the wall. Hanu could feel the ground beneath him sway from the blast, and plaster crumbled from the ceiling onto them. Then the alarm sounded. Bright lights flashed along the hallway as the siren blared. This one wasn't a drill, though. Hanu knew he would be killed if he were discovered down here like this. He ran back up the hall, but the double doors flew open and three scouts were running toward him.

Hanu panicked. Reggie and Andy weren't here to get him out of this one, and he wasn't sure if he could talk his way out of it. He reached for a door. It was locked. Then another, and it was locked, too. The third one he tried wasn't, though. He pulled the heavy door open and slipped in, then he put all his weight on it to close it back. He leaned against the door, closing his eyes and bracing himself, waiting.

"What is this?" said a wispy voice from somewhere inside the room.

Chapter Ten

The Offer

Maybe he could still salvage the situation. Maybe if he pretended he was coming to notify the Ancient One of the nature of the emergency, he could slip away undetected while they scrambled to secure the runaway prisoners. He opened his eyes, prepared to bluff.

The creature was wearing a scope over its eye and holding a scalpel and fork. It stood over a body that was strapped to a surgery table, and a light was beaming down on them. Hanu couldn't pull it off. The sheer terror on his face gave him away.

"A scout never runs from an emergency, nor is it capable of such an emotional response," the creature said. It gently put down the tools and removed its headgear. "So who are you?"

Hanu could do nothing but look at the table. Whoever it was being operated on, it wasn't human. It didn't look like anything upstairs, and it definitely didn't look like anything Hanu had ever seen in the Tome. Its orange body had tufts of hair here and there and its feline face was looking up at the ceiling. Was it… *awake*?

"Oh, don't mind my guest here," the Ancient One said. "You see, I don't prefer to watch the Bowl. There's no real reward in watching others compete for a title. I prefer a more tangible reward, harvested by my own hands."

Hanu heard another voice now- *Come to me... quickly... wait at the door.* Hanu was feeling the heaviness again. He searched for the door handle behind him now. He most definitely wouldn't be waiting at the door.

"This is the type of game I like to play," it continued. "This game also requires a great deal of strategy. I've promised this race a cure to the mysterious disease they've recently suffered from, which I *will* deliver. I created the disease, so naturally, I already have the antidote. But while I have such a fine specimen, I might as well reward myself with some genetic material, right? There's a great deal of permission involved in accessing the higher records and codes."

The creature made no advance toward Hanu. He leaned in on the patient while he spoke, stroking its face tenderly. Hanu turned the handle and made to run for it, but he was tackled back into the room by a scout. From the floor, he could see that people were running up the hallway now and someone had stopped the alarm. He realized now that the Ancient had been calling for help. He was instructing the scout to wait at the door for him. He struggled fruitlessly against the scout as he closed the door again.

"You are a very good imitation, but you're no scout. Again I'll ask, who *are* you?" came the wispy voice.

Hanu knew he was caught. There was no way out of this one. Maybe Andy had something in his bag of tricks for this type of situation, but he was long gone by now. He knew they would soon figure out the secret to his transformation. Maybe if he could take the necklace off and hide it somewhere they wouldn't discover it. He reached for it and snatched it off, returning to himself again. But the scout was too fast- he grabbed the device from his hands. He tossed it over to the Ancient One, who held it up to the light.

"This is a clever device," he said. "I shall have to kill the person who made it."

Hanu knew he messed up now. It wasn't safe to use the cloak anymore, and the others wouldn't know that. He tried to overpower the scout, as Titanya had, but his body was exhausted. It was no use.

Just then, the same councilman from earlier came in and shut the door behind him. He pulled up a couple of chairs and sat in one.

"Release the boy," he said with an air of urgency. He gestured toward the other seat expectantly. Hanu was at the mercy of this man now. He got up from the floor and sat, just barely, at the edge of the seat. The man looked at Hanu with sympathetic eyes as he leaned in, sitting on the edge of his own seat now.

"You poor boy," he said. "Look at what the Dissenters have done to you."

"I don't know any Dissenters," Hanu said stubbornly.

"So you're telling me you've come here all alone today?" he said, mock impressed. Hanu didn't want to answer that. He'd already given away Reggie and Andy's cloak, the least he could do was keep his mouth shut about anything else. Or better yet, lie.

“I did. I wanted my friends out, so I came and got them by myself. Nobody else wanted to help me,” he said, looking at the man’s golden sandals.

“I don’t think you did,” he said. “I think the Dissenters took advantage of a poor, confused and unfortunately, unstable, boy. You were hurt and scared after that unfortunate accident and they came and found you. They fed you lies to confuse you, Hanu.”

“How do you know my name?”

“I was the one who requested you. We had been putting together some research to find solutions for your paranoia and delusions, and badly need your help. You see, sometimes the radiation in the atmosphere- a little gift from our warring forefathers- can affect the child in utero. That’s what causes these psychological phenomena, which must be making life a horror for you. Poor boy, I want to help you.”

Hanu sat back in his chair, shaking his leg now.

“So what kind of research were you going to do?”

“Just some harmless bloodwork is all,” he said. “We’ve figured out the formula to correct the anomaly.”

“So I just had to take some medicine and see if it worked?” Hanu asked.

“Of course. And you know what, Hanu? I believe it does work,” he said, shaking his leg now too. “Oh, Hanu, but they fed you all of those lies about us. I think you would have been healed by now and already back home with your mom and little sister. I'm so sorry they took advantage of you."

Hanu's mind was reeling. He could have been home by now with his mom. Is it possible he was believing and acting on delusions? Had he been mistaken this whole time?

Boom. Boom.

Explosions. Had they come back for him? Hanu looked around. No windows. He couldn't tell what was going on out there. They wouldn't know where he was now, if they had come back.

Boom.

The councilman didn't pay much attention. He didn't move to secure Hanu or send any orders. He would have at least sent the scout to deal with it.

Because they were fireworks, Hanu realized. And his heart sank. Nobody was coming for him.

"I'm. so. sorry. they. took. advantage. of. you," the man repeated in a rhythmic, monotonous voice.

Hanu thought back to when he met Harris. "*I know a place you can go*," he had said. And maybe Sadie caught on to what he was doing- *you followed him here to get to us, didn't you?*"

It was ultimately Hanu's decision to run away, though- to come back and try to save the others. But he was acting on the information they had given him. Did they count on him doing that? His palms began to sweat as his mind debated itself. He wiped them on his pants. Then man was running his own hands on his white pants as well. Was he mocking Hanu?

"Listen," the man said slowly in his dowdy tone again. Hanu leaned in, hanging on to his every word. "I'm. so. sorry. they. took. advantage. of. you."

Hanu started crying. Maybe he *had* been taken advantage of. After all, Reggie and Andy just left him here. He suddenly felt isolated, helpless. Nobody was coming to save him. His gut wrenched. The councilman leaned in, too, and grabbed Hanu's shoulder reassuringly.

"Don't worry, Hanu. That's what we're here for. I forgive you." And he started again, "We. can. help. you. Okay? Trust me. We. can. help. you."

Then the man straightened back up in his chair.

"Now, feel free to tell us where your friends are hiding, Hanu. You can feel safe to tell us anything that you know about them," he said.

Hanu, who had stopped crying, licked his lips. "Well... they're from regular places in the city," he started, dazedly. And then he became uncomfortably aware of eyes on him. Hanu cut his eyes from the Ancient One to the scout, who were standing behind the councilman. They waited, quietly, listening as the two talked. Hanu noticed that the man also cut his eyes, looking behind Hanu. The man was copying him. Hanu coughed, and so did he. Then he scratched his face, and the man did, too. Something strange was happening here.

"Go on, who are they? The Dissenters? Where are they- in the city?" he asked. The man's demeanor had changed now. His eyes were cold again. Hanu thought about Akesh and the others- how the man used such a sweet and innocent voice to get them to cooperate earlier. Then he wanted to send Titanya downstairs to suffer the same fate as the twins. This man didn't care about any of them. And the Ancient clearly had no problem coercing anybody to get what he wanted.

Hanu stood up. He didn't know how, but he had to get away from here. The councilman stood up, too, and squeezed his shoulder as he did earlier. That feeling in his gut came back immediately. Hanu was helpless again. The man pulled him into a hug.

"There, there. Don't worry, as soon as you tell us everything we can go ahead and give you the medicine. Then you'll be on your way home," he said in his sweet voice again.

"Shove it," Hanu said, pushing away from him.

The man had been manipulating him the whole time. Hanu made a last attempt for the door, even though he knew he was too weak and slow to pull the heavy thing open in enough time to get away. And the man was already on him, bringing his fist down on the side of Hanu's face.

ஐஐஐஐஐஐஐ

Hanu awoke in a metal room. Ironically, it was one of the cells he had helped so many others escape from some time earlier. He sat up, rubbing the side of his head, and noticed that his arm was wrapped. He tore through the bandage. Two scabbed holes, but no red blemish. They may have drawn blood or perhaps given a few injections of medicine, but they didn't bother putting another trade in him. He looked through the mesh door, careful not to touch it.

"Anyone there?"

No answer. He looked across the hall and saw that the cells were empty. It looked like they hadn't recovered many of the escaped prisoners, he thought. He laid back down, too tired to think hard. He would rest for a while longer then come up with a plan.

Hanu closed his eyes and listened. There were occasional footsteps and people talking in the distance. He wondered what they planned on doing with him. He busted out most of their test subjects, put a hole in their wall and who knows what Reggie blew up for the diversion. He was surprised they didn't override him on the spot.

Hanu thought about Akesh and the others. He wondered if they had made it back to Deprogramming by now. Ester was probably ecstatic to see Jeremiah. He wondered if she'd go back to being a hermit now that he was there to hermit with. Had they moved on to the Underground without him? Well, probably not with Paula testing them first. He smirked to himself. Hopefully they would be able to just move on to the Underground and be happy. Hanu wasn't able to do that, and this is where it landed him. But still, if he were going to die, at least he saved a few others.

Hours later, the man came, holding a tray. He squeezed into the room and sat down in front of Hanu.

"I'm afraid we started off on the wrong foot," he said, pushing the tray towards Hanu. "My name is Aric."

He had brought food- rice and a bowl of soup, a bunch of grapes and a cup of water. Hanu drank down the soup and started on the rice before Aric could invite him to eat. It had been so long since Hanu had a meal.

“Hanu, no matter what it seems to you, the Ancients are here to restore the order that they originally intended for us to enjoy. The methods may seem cruel to you, but they are necessary,” he said. Hanu listened with a mouthful of rice. His belly was full and warm.

“You don’t understand because you’re just a child. War, disease, senseless killing, and hate- you’ve never had to experience such things, thanks to the Ancients.”

Hanu was feeling giddy now, intoxicated. He grabbed a couple of grapes and popped them in his mouth. Then he shoved a few in Aric’s face.

“Oh, no thank you. But if you’re ready to tell me how I can find your friends, I’d like to help them. They’re sick and they can really use your help right now.”

Hanu thought about the Bathtub Resort. He could see it clearly in his mind now- the secret door, the tunnel, the luminescent doorway. They were all so wonderful. He wanted to tell Aric all about them. He just knew he was going to spill the beans. But he tried not to. Hanu tried to think of something else, anything else. Then he blurted out.

“I used to be afraid of the dark. I was twelve before I could sleep without a night light.”

It was working. He just had to force himself to think about anything besides Deprogramming.

"When I was little I used to pretend I was an Ancient. I would fly around on a spaceship- which was really just my mom's couch-"

"The Dissenters, who are they? What are their names?" Aric asked impatiently.

Hanu tried harder now to keep his mind busy. He kept going. "I ate six jalapenos one time at the Flush and later on that night I had diarrhea. I ended up accidentally pooping myself because Mr. Beady took too long unlocking the door," he admitted, laughing aloud.

Aric stood up and kicked the tray out of the cell. It splattered against the opposite cell, sending rice and grapes all over the place. Then he slammed the door and stormed off. After his footsteps faded Hanu laid back down and continued listening the low hum of the door.

For the next three days Aric came with a bowl of soup and rice. Hanu ate the rice and politely turned down the soup each day. Then on the fourth day, Aric brought a bowl of rice with the soup mixed in and reassured Hanu that he would need to keep his strength up for the trip home. After Hanu refused it Aric left the cell, tight lipped, and didn't come back. Later, a scout came with a loaf of stale bread and a cup of water, which Hanu ate cautiously.

That night the citizen's anthem played over the loud speaker. First it was low, so Hanu wasn't sure what it was. He could tell it was a woman's voice- different from everyone else he'd been hearing. He thought maybe the secretary had come up to deliver some news. He lifted his head off the cold floor just enough to get a good listen.

Chapter Ten

I promise integrity and support to my brethren

Of the world and of my homeland.

I will follow the words of the council,

Who are guided by the Ancient Ones.

Every day, I look to my leaders

To bestow wisdom and knowledge

It is in their care that I place my life

And the future of all the world.

Hanu must've said this anthem thousands of times in his life. Everyone was required to learn it in their first year of school, and recite it every morning before instruction started. He remembered how they made a big deal about it when he still hadn't gotten it right by the end of his first year. They wanted to retain him, just for that. And for that reason, he despised it. He hated it even more now that they were playing it nonstop. Every time it started over, the voice got louder.

He put his head back down and curled into a fetal position, covering his ears. The sound of the woman's voice seeped through his palms, but it was bearable. He fell asleep somewhere around the twenty fifth rendition of it.

Hanu started counting his days, more or less, by stale loaves of bread. He was currently working on his fourth loaf, so they had been playing the anthem for about that long now, he figured. Sometimes it was played very low, so it was just another background noise, and other times it blared so loudly Hanu couldn't hear himself scream. Then the voice would gradually slow so that the anthem would be drawn out. Just when Hanu was starting to think that time was slowing down it would jump back to regular speed, making him nauseous.

In order to keep himself from going insane he would hum loudly or sing different songs at the top of his lungs. He tried to think about anything besides the stupid anthem. He found himself wishing that the other beings that he saw in the Tome of the Earth would come and save him. If he could just fall asleep maybe he could ask them for help.

“Why don’t you help me!” he would scream at the top of his lungs.

Sometimes he would get up and dance wildly. Eventually he got the idea to rip off bits of his shirt and stuff them in his ears. It improved Hanu’s existence considerably, though he still wasn’t able to concentrate enough to formulate an escape plan.

On the fifth day the anthem stopped and Aric came back.

“Are you ready to cooperate? I spoke with your mother and she said she was ready for you to come home, Hanu. Aren’t you ready to go home now?”

Hanu stared at him blankly. He thought about darting through the open cell door, but he knew there was probably a scout somewhere in the hall.

“Poor boy, you must be tired of these conditions. The sooner you give us the information we need, the sooner you can get out of here. What do you say?”

Chapter Ten

Hanu licked his dry lips and cleared his throat. Then he finally spoke. "I promise integrity and support to my brethren, of the world and of my homeland. I will follow the words-"

Aric kicked him in the stomach, sending stale bread into his throat. Hanu doubled over and allowed his face to rest on the cold floor. He stayed there, trying not to show how much pain he felt. He continued.

"...of the council, who are guided by the Ancient Ones. Every day, I look to my leaders, to bestow wisdom and knowledge."

When he looked up again Aric had gone. Hanu wondered just how long he could resist. He crawled into a corner and hugged his knees. That night bread didn't come.

The next morning, two scouts escorted him upstairs. They offered no explanation when they came into his cell and picked him up off the floor. Once on his feet, he allowed them to guide him to the elevators. He thought maybe they were taking him for override, which he wouldn't have minded too much. At least this way what little information he had would go with him to his grave, if they gave him one, and the Underground would be safe. They passed through the third floor lobby, which was eerily similar to the one on the first floor, and through a set of doors on the other side.

They left him in a large windowless room. It was empty, except for a single chair placed at the center. He decided to sit and wait for whatever it was that would happen next. After a while, a voice came over the speaker system. The same woman who had recited the citizen's anthem before.

"Humanity, left to its own devices, can only create inequity."

And then Hanu was submerged in a silent movie. The sun beat down on him from somewhere up above. It was so bright he could almost feel the warmth. He stood up, adjusting his eyes. There was a shack made of mud and straw, surrounded by cracked earth. In the doorway of the shack, a child was playing with a doll made from the same straw as the roof. Her arms and legs were nothing more than sticks, and her belly was distended. He watched her play contentedly with the doll for a while.

Then Hanu was in a more familiar place- a restaurant. Three men were laughing with each other, rubbing paunchy stomachs. A woman came by and collected their plates of food and threw them in the trash.

"These aren't the only atrocities that we have made for ourselves," the woman said. And now Hanu was looking over a large body of water. The surface of the water was streaked with black gunk in places, and dead animals floated in clusters along the shore. After that, Hanu was in a dark and littered alley. A man was walking quickly down the alley with his faced tucked in his coat. Two men approached him from the rear. Hanu screamed as he was kicked to the ground and robbed- he forgot it was just a movie.

Next, Hanu was sitting in the cockpit of an airplane. Two men smiled at each other as they dropped a missile over a beautiful city. The missile glided toward the city as people below scrambled to escape the blast. It didn't detonate, though, because a silvery globular craft came from thin air and beamed it away.

"That is why the Ancients were forced to step in. They came to save us from our own self destruction," she said.

Chapter Ten

Then Hanu was surrounded by faces- happy faces of people who had been saved from the blast, and starving children holding food, and a sickly woman taking medicine. Some of the people cried tears of joy or jumped in the air. They were chanting and dancing because of the Ancient Ones.

"People like you and I will never understand the horrors of the past- war, starvation, poverty. It's thanks to the Ancient Ones, who are our creators and saviors. We have only to correct our path and heal the scars of our history."

Hanu found himself back at the Flush. It looked just as it had the last time he was there. It may have even been his own unit. It was hard to tell, as they all looked alike. A patient, who Hanu had never seen before, was attacking a staff member.

"Delusions, schizophrenia, hallucinations, and paranoia are our last conquest."

He could see another patient, in her room, sitting in a corner and pulling her own hair out. She was screaming in distress.

"We work diligently to help those children who have fallen victim to the ghosts of the past," she said. Then the scene changed. He saw his mother in the lab downstairs, extracting blood from a little boy. Hanu was unnerved. His own mother had been here.

"Your mother completed her practicum here, at this very facility. She understands the importance of your mental health and the health of all the children of the world."

Then Hanu could see hundreds of children, holding hands and singing. They were at some sort of celebration. Hanu could see the Ancients in the background looking on as they sang. Then the scene changed again, startling Hanu. This scene showed an Ancient One pulling a child out of some rubble. The small boy was bleeding from somewhere behind his hairline. Hanu could see that an apartment building had been blown apart.

"The Dissenters do what they can to disturb the peace that this new era has brought. At any cost, they tear down the order that the Ancient Ones brought to Earth in order to establish a new era of fear. They use deception- taking advantage of our delicate and impressionable youth."

Now three teenagers burned down a field of corn. One of them sprayed a liquid onto the crops while another ignited a torch and threw it in. They ran off, laughing, as it exploded.

"They spread false information in order to coerce our young to carry out their missions, but they don't tell them the real objectives that they are working toward."

Then Hanu was at a Food Distribution Center. He could see that the line had backed up, and panicked citizens were banging on the doors. These people were the ones who suffered from the crops being burned down.

"The time to choose is upon you, Hanu. Will you live with us, or die with the Dissenters?"

Finally he was back in the empty room. He wasn't sure how to feel after seeing what he saw. The scouts silently escorted him back to his cell and left him to think.

Chapter Ten

Hanu went back and forth in his mind. He *felt* sound. He felt like he was making the best decisions he could, given everything that he'd witnessed since he left the Flush, but he was faltering. He thought about Reggie and Andy. Are they the Dissenters? And had they lied to him? Was Paula a Dissenter, too? He didn't want to do terrible things to innocent people. He just wanted to live in peace, and help others do the same. Maybe he would live in peace if he cooperated, he thought. They would let him go home to his mom and sister.

But what about mom, he argued with himself. He saw her sticking needles into an unconscious boy. How could she be so cruel? He could ask the same of her. Were the Ancient Ones lying to her to get her to do all those awful things? Aric, the Ancient Ones- *they* were deceitful. Paula was crude at times, but she never used sweet words or shady tactics to get what she wanted.

Hanu wondered how bad it would be to just give up. The Ancient Ones have all the power. And maybe they were right. Maybe after he took the medicine, he would suddenly realize how foolish he'd been. Hanu screamed in frustration. He would never know the truth, so he couldn't trust himself to make the right decision.

That night, the door opened again. He looked up, expecting stale bread, but instead it was one of the twins. He didn't want to believe what he was seeing. The boy looked to be in considerably better condition than the last time Hanu saw them. He wore crisp, clean clothes and his hair was combed. He smelled a whole lot better, too, and what's more, he brought a feast. Hanu eyed the tray suspiciously. It held a steak dinner with mashed potatoes and gravy, peas, a salad, a cup of juice and a large slice of pie.

"It's for you," he said. "Hanu, right? I'm La. I heard you tried to rescue me. Thanks for that."

"I'm sorry I didn't do a better job of it. I should've come sooner," Hanu said. "What are you doing here, anyway?"

"I'm bringing you dinner. Go ahead, it's yours," La said, pushing the tray closer to Hanu. "I came to give you a message, too."

"Oh yeah, what's the message?" Hanu asked, eating a handful of peas.

"Things are a lot better for us here now since the day you tried to rescue us. We were really angry, but the Ancients helped us to see how good life can be, Hanu. We're happy here now, and all we had to do was cooperate," La said.

Hanu stopped eating the food. "This is a trick."

"No, no trick," he said. Picking up the steak and taking a few bites. He offered Hanu the rest. "We eat like this every day now- as much as we want! And we have real bedrooms, too. They let us stay in the palace now and everything."

"La, they're experimenting on people here. They're trying to take over our planet. We have to fight them. Remember what your brother said? They're liars," Hanu urged.

He was appalled. The twins have given up. They've been broken by the Council's tactics. If those two hard knocks could be swayed then what chance did Hanu have?

"If they are, then it's probably for the best," La said, playing with the mashed potatoes now. "Hanu, please do yourself a favor and just give up. They're offering to send you home and pardon everything you've done. Me and Tui- we don't have parents, but they've given us a home. They treat us like royalty now. They'll help *you* if you help *them*."

Hanu looked at La in disbelief. He had no more words. He was tired of trying to find words- words to think with and words to defend himself with.

"They'll be coming for you in the morning. That's your offer, so just think about it," he said, standing up now. He handed the plate to Hanu. "Oh, yeah. Try the gravy. It's delicious."

Hanu looked at the plate. In the gravy there were three words: *Tonight we escape.*

Chapter Eleven

An orchestrated Effort

Hanu had been waiting for hours, but still no sign of anything unusual. He was starting to wonder if La could follow through on his word. Or maybe he tried to escape, but was caught. Would he hear word of the attempt? Well, the assistants had already gone home for the night, so there was no one at the front desk to overhear gossiping. The only company he had to look forward to was the scout who patrolled the building. Every once and a while he would enter, silently take a turn up and down the hall, then leave.

He listened hard anyway. Maybe he'd hear some explosions or a siren to indicate that things were happening. He just hoped that events were being set in motion. Hanu could hear another prisoner cough or sniffle from time to time, but nothing more than that. Perhaps he was supposed to get himself out of the cell and meet with them somewhere. No, that would be a stretch. He just wished the message hadn't been so vague. Just three words: tonight we escape.

It would have been helpful if La could have told him a little more information, like who he meant by 'we'. Was it just he and Hanu who would escape? Because if that were the case, odds were quite slim that it would actually happen. Or was Tui in on it too? Was Tui willing to give up all the pampering, as well? If Hanu remembered correctly, Tui was the tougher of the two, so that would definitely give them a slightly more realistic chance of escaping if he were in on it.

But even still, they needed someone who had access to resources. A couple of nine year olds, no matter how tough, wouldn't be able to outwit an entire faction of Ancients in their own fortress. Hanu doubted that they had any Underground friends that would be coming to bust them out, but that's exactly what they needed.

Just as Hanu was about to give up, he heard someone enter the chamber. It was feint, but he could distinctly hear the door swing open and then close with a gentle click. He stood up and put his face as close to the door as he could. The air grew thick with anticipation. He wasn't sure if it was his eagerness or the buzz on the door that made his hair stand on end.

Moments later the double doors slowly opened. He could hear slow and unsure footsteps. These didn't belong to the scout. Whoever it was seemed to be looking for something. They would pause occasionally before moving on a few steps more. Hanu stood up.

A few seconds later he could see that it was a woman. She wore glasses and her hair was bobbed around her face. She stopped short, startled by Hanu's appearance. He must've looked like a lunatic, standing at his door wide eyed, he thought.

"Hanu?"

"Who are you?" he asked cautiously.

"My name is Celia. I'm a surrogate. I take care of the twins," she said more urgently now, looking back up the hall. "We have to get you out of here quickly. I sent the scout to the fifth floor, but he'll probably be back soon."

Celia tried to pull at the door but she jumped back, shocked. She reared back to kick it down but Hanu stopped her.

"No, no, no! Just hit the button and open the door, don't bother with all of that. The controls are down there," he pointed.

Celia trotted down the hallway to the console at the end. He could hear her playing with the knobs. She turned the buzz off, so he leaned against the mesh to see better, but then she turned it back on and shocked him.

"Which one?" she whispered urgently down the hall.

"Don't worry about the knobs- use the buttons to open the doors. Just hit them all." Hanu didn't remember now which set of buttons actually opened the cells. Andy was the operator during their rescue mission.

Then Hanu heard the cell doors open, one at a time. He shook with excitement. When his finally slid open, he took a nervous step into the hallway.

"Let's go," she said, grabbing him by the elbow and running through the doors.

"Someone will be in the lobby. How are we going to get past them?" he asked as they got on the elevator.

Chapter Eleven

Celia didn't answer. Instead she took a couple deep breaths and ran her hands through her hair. She looked extremely nervous, which made Hanu question whether they'd actually get away tonight. But he was out of his cell and halfway through the building, so he couldn't really complain at this point. The doors opened on the first floor.

"Delores, honey, can you get me a mop and some towels? I got sick in the elevator and I need to clean it up quickly," she said, peeking her head out into the hallway.

"Oh, Celia I told you not to eat that taco. Hold on, let me see what I've got," Delores said.

"I'm going to go to the restroom real quick, I'll be right back to clean it up. Just set the bucket by the elevator, will you?"

Hanu could hear Delores shuffle for a bit and then a door closing. She must've gone into a closet to get some cleaning materials. Then Celia beckoned for Hanu to follow as she walked out of the front doors.

Hanu was free. He looked up into the sky, and took a breath. It was the first breath of fresh air in what seemed like ages. But the moment was short lived, because she was pulling him into the shadows now. Though there were no sirens, Hanu still had to be vigilant, he realized. He followed her as she ran toward the wall. Once they were leaning up against it, she turned to Hanu.

"I'm saving you because Tui and La wouldn't leave without you. Keep up. We have to get to the residential area, and that's maybe a mile and a half away. Don't ruin this for us, *please*," she urged.

Though her words were stern, she had a caring face. Her brown eyes were warm and compassionate. She must think a lot of the twins to do this for them.

"I'll keep up," Hanu said, nodding affirmatively.

The two ran in the moonlight, keeping as tight as they could against the District wall. Hanu knew they only had so long before Delores realized Celia wasn't in the bathroom. He wondered if she would alert anyone about the strange encounter, or if she would just dismiss it. Either way, the scout would soon return to patrol duty and notice that Hanu was missing. Then an alert would be sent for sure.

Hanu had so many questions for her, but he was winded enough already. He hadn't seen this much action in a while, and his body was punishing him for it. They kept it up for quite some time, only slowing to check their bearings or to avoid scouts. He was good at that by now, though. Hanu didn't realize how large the District of Operations was. It was like a small city, with a recreation center and all.

They eventually arrived at their destination- a large house in the residential area. Celia swiped her left wrist under the doorknob, and the door clicked open. Hanu was confused.

"This is your house?" he asked.

He wasn't sure why she would be bringing him back home. Did this woman plan to keep him and the twins hidden away at her house?

"Yes it is, but we're not staying long," she said rushing through the dark. Hanu fumbled around, trying to keep up as she dropped a bag by the front door. He could hear footsteps on the staircase.

"Hanu, is that you?"

"La? Tui?"

But there was no time to talk. Celia swept them out the front door and around the side of the house. Then she went into the neighbor's garage and pulled out a Nomad. The boys ran to the vehicle as she threw the door open. Tui dove in first, followed by his brother, and Hanu jumped in last. He barely got the door closed before she was pulling forward.

Celia drove quietly through the neighborhood, with both hands on the wheel and sitting erect. Everyone was too shaken to speak, so they sat hunkered down in the back, holding their breaths. They entered the tunnel system, driving a little faster now. Hanu couldn't believe they were just driving out of the District of Operations, as if they were just off to run errands. He never could have dreamed up this type of escape. He silently took back all of the doubtful thoughts he'd had about this woman.

"It seems like everything is going as planned," she finally said.

The boys watched, wide eyed. As they approached the gate everyone sunk down as far as they could for a security read. She pulled up to the console and rolled her window down to press a button. The red laser scanned the vehicle.

"Abnormal scan. Please present access credentials," a cool, automated voice said.

Hanu could see the beads of sweat forming on Celia's forehead. She rifled through the various compartments inside the vehicle, looking for something. Then she pulled out a small key ring and inserted a square chip into the drive.

Click.

As the gate opened she looked back nervously to make sure nobody else had followed. Then she pulled out of the District of Operations and into the night. For a couple of miles they just looked out of the windows in silence. They were traveling again, escorted by a District representative. But this time it was toward freedom.

"So where are you taking us?" Hanu finally asked.

"Didn't really think that all the way through. I feel like we need to get out of the city, though. Maybe to one of the fringe cities- we can hide out there," she said.

Clearly this woman wasn't a part of the Underground, Hanu thought to himself. She didn't have a clue how fast the Council would catch them if they tried to do that. They had to get rid of the vehicle and their trades as fast as they could if they wanted a chance of survival. She had to have thought about that when she planned the escape.

Then Hanu's heart started racing. He suddenly felt panicked. He fought the urge to jump out of the vehicle and run as fast as he could away from them. He looked at Tui and La. Their contented faces shone in the moonlight. They looked at each other satisfactorily, grinning. What if this was another one of Aric's tricks? What if it was an attempt to get information on the Underground? Of course. If he was busted out, he'd naturally try to return to the Underground. All they had to do was track them down. La said it himself- the twins had given up, and all they had to do was cooperate with the Ancients and they'd be pampered for life. That's why it had been so easy to get away- not a siren, or alert, or at least one single shouting scout giving them chase. They basically strolled out of that building unhindered. Hanu felt sick. His hands started shaking, and he couldn't breathe.

"Hey you okay back there?" Celia asked.

Hanu laid down in the seat, trying to hide his alarm. He had to think clearly. This woman could be genuine. The look on her face when she told him not to ruin it for her and the twins was genuine. He could believe that, at least. She was a caring woman. He put that face in his mind, and forced himself to calm.

"Celia," he said quietly. "Why are you helping us?"

She was quiet for a moment. He couldn't tell if she was making up a lie or if she was considering how best to answer the question. He watched her gentle face twist into a frown.

"When I came back from University, I didn't really know what to do with myself. I wanted to do something I thought was meaningful, and helping children was always at the front of my mind, so I applied to be a surrogate. I've lived at the District for twelve years now, raising orphans for the Ancients. Some of them work in the District now, but others sometimes just disappear."

Celia turned down another street, checking the rearview mirror again. "I learned to not ask questions about them. I figured that I'm doing so much good for a lot of children, so a couple gone here and there shouldn't matter. But I always knew. I heard stories about where they ended up."

Her face was stern now as she decided which way to go. She was driving in circles, and they would be caught soon if they kept it up. Hanu wasn't sure if he trusted her yet, though.

"So why them? What made you decide to help the twins escape?" he asked.

"I'm just tired of it. I can't ignore the feeling in my gut anymore. It's just eating away at me, you know? I don't want to be involved in all this anymore; I want to be free. And I want the twins to be free. When they brought them to us they said it would be temporary- that we were to clean them up and pamper them before they went for override."

Tui and La grimaced at each other. Apparently they didn't know that bit. "I told you, La," Tui said.

"Well if you didn't know they were going to override you, why did you want to get away?" Hanu asked La. "Why give it all up?"

"He's my brother. He sticks with me because I protect him. Always have, and always will," Tui said proudly as he poked a thumb into his chest. La conceded to his brother's claim by nodding agreeably.

"And I just know that these Ancients are full of baloney. I can *feel* it."

"Well said," Celia agreed, smiling.

Chapter Eleven

Hanu was as satisfied as time would permit, because now there were lights off in the distance, approaching them. A Convoy.

"Hey, we need to ditch the vehicle," he said urgently. "You need to drive faster. Do you know where the Bathtub Resort is? It's a bar in the Entertainment District."

"Yeah, I know it."

"Get us close to there, but not too close. We'll leave the Nomad and run the rest of the way," he said. The twins groaned at the thought.

Celia was driving like a madwoman now, looking in her rear view mirror. The twins crouched back down in the seat now as the Nomad silently moved down the metal street.

"So what's at the Bathtub Resort?" she asked over her shoulder. Hanu wasn't sure how much he should tell, though. He knew they needed to get rid of their trades, but he still didn't trust that he could take them to Paula.

"Someone who will keep us hidden," he said.

He would talk to Toni first and ask for his advice on what to do next. Toni was one of the experts, so he would decide if they should be granted passage or not.

"So you guys were just going to drive off and hope to not get caught?" Hanu asked, looking out of the back window. The lights were further away now, but he knew they were tracking the vehicle. They needed to mislead whoever was in that Convoy.

"Well I thought we'd be long gone by the time they noticed we were missing. Plus, my neighbor is gone for the next four days. I didn't think they would notice his vehicle was missing until he got back. I had a pretty good plan, you know."

"No complaints here," Hanu said. "Are we close yet?"

"Maybe three miles or so."

Hanu started looking for places to ditch the Nomad- an alley, the front of a supply store, a dimly lit park space. If only they had one of Harris' scramblers they wouldn't have to move so frantically. They were approaching the outskirts of the business district and getting ready to cross over into the entertainment side of town when Hanu thought about it.

"The courtyard! Get us to that courtyard with that statue in it!" he said, shaking her shoulder wildly.

"The Fountain of Hope?"

"Yes! Get close. Park at one of those shopping centers," he said, pulling one of the twins up from the floor. "When we stop, get ready to run to the fountain."

Celia pulled the Nomad right onto the sidewalk in the middle of a shopping center. The boutiques and shops abutted one another without break, so they had to run along the brightly lit windows to find a way through to the park behind. Celia found a narrow alley, and they squeezed through into the shadows.

"Where are we going?" Tui asked.

"There's something here. Or, it was here," Hanu said, leading them through the bushes. He had nothing more than the moonlight to guide him. He could see off to the north- a trellis. “Come on!”

Hanu was on his hands and knees now, sweeping under the bushes. It had to be here. He could see lights off in the distance, winding through the courtyard. The Convoy again. Celia pulled the twins further behind the trellis.

“What are you looking for, Hanu?” Celia asked.

“This.”

He was holding up a smooth, round rock to the light.

“It’s a scrambler. They can’t locate us by your trades anymore,” Hanu said, smiling. He sat down next to the twins and leaned up against the trellis. They watched as the Convoy drove around the shopping plaza.

ஜஜஜஜஜஜஜ

An hour later they were standing outside of the Bathtub Resort. Hanu got a strong sense of déjà vu as he approached the narrow doorway. He knocked three times and took a step back. Toni *should* be here, he thought. He remembered the last time he was at the Bathtub Resort the old man said he stayed all night to take care of business related things. Hanu was sure that this was the very business he was talking about.

Nothing.

He knocked again. Tonight of all nights, Toni had to be here. Celia and the twins hid behind the marquee. He could see that they were growing anxious now. They had no vehicle and no plan, and the Council was already after them. They were in way over their heads. Hanu decided they should get off of the sidewalk- get to a more hidden spot and wait it out until morning. He turned to walk away when the door cracked. It was Toni.

"What do you want?"

"It's me, Hanu. Remember me? Harris brought me here a few weeks ago. We got the Harriet-"

"I remember you," he said in a hollow voice. "I don't serve after hours anymore. Sorry, guys."

Hanu moved in closer to the door. "Why? What happened?"

"It's too dangerous nowadays," he said before he closed the door. "I'm sure you can find another way."

Hanu looked over to the others. Celia was looking up and down the street nervously now, cupping the twins under her arms as if it would hide them.

Hanu failed. That was the last trick he had. But at least they had the scrambler. He led them into the alley behind the Bathtub Resort.

"We have to think," Hanu said.

"Just how was this man going to hide us?" Tui asked, eyeing the building.

Hanu figured he owed them at least a little more information. "The Council will always be able to track us down by our trades, and we can't always rely on this scrambler. We need to remove them and become invisible.

That's the best way to hide," he said, looking from Celia to the boys.

"And that man would've done that?" she asked.

"Yes, but apparently he's not in the business anymore. I wonder what's going on."

"Isn't there anyone else who could do it?"

Hanu was racking his brain. It's not like he knew a whole heck of a lot of people as it was. And he didn't know anyone besides Toni who actually did the surgery. But maybe Harris would know of someone else who could.

"We'll have to do a lot of walking tonight. We need to take advantage of the darkness and get where we need to go," he said, talking more to himself than the others.

He knew he could get them to Harris' house from here. Hanu remembered the way since they were forced to walk so slowly the last time. Would he mind Hanu showing up on his doorstep in the middle of the night?

"I know a person who might know how to get it done. He's our only hope now."

So they set off slowly, cautiously, through the streets towards the Residential District. He was looking for the building with a bronze statue out front. Their vigilance paid off, though, as they knocked on Harris' door just before sunrise.

"Lookey here!" Harris said as he threw the door open. He pulled Hanu into the apartment, and the others filed behind. "I thought you were gone by now, what happened?"

"I ran into some trouble," Hanu said sheepishly.

Harris was more serious now. He bit his lip as he looked at the others. "Hanu, you should have stayed put. It's not safe anymore."

"I heard. We went to the Bathtub Resort and Toni said he wasn't serving anymore. What's going on?"

Harris walked over to the window and peeked out. "Was that you during the Bowl, then? You went back for the twins?"

"Well, yes. But I was caught. Been there ever since. But Celia helped us bust out," Hanu said, smiling at Celia. Harris pulled a large box from under his coffee table and opened it. There were different colored gemstones and crystals in it as well as several darker ones. It was a rock collection.

"So you guys all have your trades, I presume," he said testily. Hanu knew he had inconvenienced Harris by coming here.

"I had that covered," Hanu said, putting the scrambler on the table. Harris picked it up and rolled it in his hands, laughing.

"You're a resourceful one, aren't you?"

"Harris, we just need to get them removed. Do you know anyone else that can help us?" Hanu asked.

"I do," he said, looking at Celia. "Does she know everything?"

"Celia?" Hanu asked. He was embarrassed to say he didn't trust her enough to tell her everything. "Well, I figured I'd leave that to someone else, actually. I'm not in the position to really say anything."

"Smart boy," Harris said, putting his shoes on.

"What do you mean, *everything*?" Celia asked indignantly.

"Sorry to keep you in the dark, but being as things are the way they are…" Harris said as he tied his shoes. Then he grabbed a bag and put a loaf of bread in it. "How do we know we can we trust you?"

At this, the twins interjected. "She saved us. Celia would never do anything to hurt us!" Tui said.

"Yeah, she ran away with us. She left her whole life behind and everything," La added.

"What do you think?" Harris said, looking at Hanu. He was honored that Harris thought so highly of his opinion, but he really didn't trust himself to judge it.

"I'm just… I think so, but… I don't know," he admitted, looking down at his shoes.

"Well what do the voices say?" Harris asked with a wry smile. Hanu smiled, too. Celia cut in, angry now.

"Look guys, I may not have had the best plan, but I had good intentions. I don't know what you guys mean by 'everything', but as long as the twins and I can be together and safe, I don't care. I'm not a spy or anything like that, if that's what you're thinking, so whatever illegal operation you guys have going on, I don't care as long as it gets us as far away from the district as possible!"

At that, Harris took a final glance out of the window. "Alright. That settles that, then. Let's go."

They were walking up the street now, as casually as they could. It wasn't unusual for a couple of people to be walking through the neighborhood at dawn, so they blended well enough. And if the Council was locating them by their trades, they were covered.

"You know the little coffeehouse across from the elementary school down here?" Harris asked Celia.

"You mean Halgoria Reform?"

"No, there's another school," he said. "It's further up the road here, and there's this pink coffeehouse across from it. It's on Hopkins Street."

"You mean Neoma Prep?" Celia asked. "That Coffeehouse is not pink, dude. It's purple."

"I'm a man. Why should I worry about all these delicate color distinctions?" Harris argued playfully. "You knew what I was talking about, right?"

"Everyone knows the difference between pink and purple!" La chimed in.

"Here, let me open this chartreuse door for you," Harris said, bowing and pretending to open the door of a supply store.

"That door is blue. Chartreuse is nowhere near blue, just so you know," she laughed.

"Whatever," Harris said, laughing now, too. "Anyway, that coffeehouse down there-"

"It's called Tantra Coffeehouse," Hanu interjected. He remembered it. He would pass by it every day on his way to school. He remembered smelling the fresh coffee. It smelled so good, and it always reminded him that he would soon be in class. It sort of got him 'in the zone' every day. And he always wondered what kind of name that was- Tantra. It was painted inside of a lotus flower on a large sign in the front of the building.

"Yeah, that one. You from around here, kid?" Harris asked.

"Yeah, so we better lay low. Someone might recognize me," Hanu answered, walking closer behind Harris now.

Harris put his arm around Hanu and pulled him into a half hug as they walked. "Well anyway, Tantra is where we're going. When we get there you'll order the Harriet. Three of them with lemon, okay?" he said to Celia.

Hanu smiled now. He was happy to see Harris again, and even better, he didn't have to drink that stuff again. The twins were not going to happy, though, he thought to himself, laughing. He grabbed Harris tighter as they walked down the street.

"You know Harris, you should come with us," Hanu suggested, looking up at the man's tired face. The familiar smell of oregano wafted from his sleeve. "You said yourself that things are getting bad here."

"Yeah, it is getting tight here. We thought maybe the Council knew something at first. They came in and beat Toni up pretty bad. Tore up the place, too, looking for something. But it turned out they hit up every joint in the Entertainment District. It was random, but Toni decided it wasn't worth it. He's laying low now."

"And you?"

"Well it's not like I have a whole heck of a lot to do with anything. Well, I guess I do know a few things, but I don't think I'm really a major player here."

"How do you guys know each other?" Tui asked.

"Well, actually, when the Convoy flipped and we all ran our separate ways, I ended up hiding in a pile of garbage," Hanu said. "And Harris found me."

"And it was gross," Harris said, squirming. The twins were laughing at Hanu now.

"So how about it, Harris, why don't you come with us?" Hanu pressed.

"Look sharp, guys," Celia said, looking up at the holographic trees they were passing. She was trying to hide her face from a Convoy that was driving slowly past them now. If they weren't laughing it up they would have noticed before. It slowly drove by, but didn't stop. Maybe they didn't recognize them.

"You know what guys, we should probably move faster," Harris said, picking up his pace.

Hanu wasn't quite sure that they had gotten away. Harris hid a grimace behind a half-hearted smile as he ushered them across the street, grabbing one of the twins as they went. They ducked into an alley that came out on the other side of the block.

"We should be okay if we don't come across any more of those things," Harris said as they walked past a public park space.

Chapter Eleven

Hanu could see the elementary school off in the distance now. They were close. They passed a couple of people, here and there, but there was really nobody around to blend in with. As they crossed the street another Convoy drove behind them, a little faster than the first one. There was no mistaking it. They were spotted.

They ducked behind an apartment complex, hoping to lose it, but when they came out on the other side, another Convoy was coming around the corner. It stopped, and a group of scouts got out. They ducked back into the alley behind the apartment building.

"Celia, get these kids over to the Coffeehouse. I'm gonna hold them off for a while."

"Harris, you can't do that! They'll take you into the district," Hanu argued, but Harris cut him off.

"I haven't done anything wrong, Hanu. I'll say you guys asked me for directions and then I'll throw them off the trail. Trust me."

Hanu had a bad feeling about it, though. He knew that they'd been seen and that the scouts wouldn't be nice about it. He tried to pull Harris further into the alley.

"Harris, they'll torture you," Hanu pleaded.

"You know what," Harris said, watching the scouts march up the street. "After I deal with these guys, I think I *will* retire. I'll meet you at the coffeehouse and we'll go to the Underground together, okay?"

Hanu nodded his head. He knew he wasn't going to win, so he let the man go. Harris nodded at the group and turned onto the sidewalk to meet the scouts.

They were saying something to him now. Hanu couldn't hear it. Then Harris held his arms out, saying something back.

"Come on, let's go," Celia whispered. But just as he was turning to go, he saw one scout rear back and punch Harris in the gut, sending him to the ground. Hanu wanted to scream, but she had already put a hand over his mouth and was pulling him back into the alley. Hanu fought as the twins grabbed his arms, wide eyed.

"We have to get out of here," one of them whispered. But Hanu couldn't just leave Harris now. He was the one who saved Hanu in the first place- and he helped his friends get to the Underground. Harris was a good person, and he was finally going to go to the Underground, himself, to be free.

Two of the other scouts picked him off the ground and the first one was kicking him in the face now. His blood pooled on the sidewalk in a dark puddle. Hanu struggled against Celia and the twins. The scouts were killing Harris, and they just wanted him to walk away like it was nothing. Hanu tried to get to him, to save him, but he was overpowered. Celia slapped Hanu in the face.

"Snap out of it!" she said. "Just snap out of it, Hanu. He knew it was dangerous going out there like that, but he risked it to save you. If you have any decency you'll do what he asked you to do. The worst way to disgrace his sacrifice is to go out there and get yourself caught!"

Chapter Eleven

Hanu yielded. He stopped struggling and allowed Celia to pull him down the alley. He didn't really care what happened anymore. They had done so much to him already. How could it get any worse? After all they've done- separated him from his family, tried to experiment on him, hunted him down and tortured him- they went further. How could they excuse the fact that they beat a man to death outside of an apartment building in broad daylight?

The Coffeehouse was just around the corner. Celia pulled Hanu past the school, his school. Teachers were walking up the steps leading to the entrance and children were taking turns on the swing-set before the morning bell rang. People were going on with their everyday activities, unaware of what was happening to an innocent man just a block away. They bolted across the street and through the glass door. The barista, who had been cleaning glasses with a small cloth, helped Hanu into a seat.

"Hey, we need three Harriets, with lemon," Celia said, looking through the window.

"Uh, let me get the boss," the woman said, wringing the towel in her hands. She disappeared into the back room quietly.

A few minutes later a man with sandy hair and blue eyes came around the bar. He wore a T-shirt and cargo shorts with sandals. He hardly looked like he would be anyone's boss.

"Hi, I'm Adam. How can I help you?" he asked, smiling candidly.

Celia, who had gotten her composure back by now, stood up and crossed the room. "Hi' I'm Celia. My friends and

I here need help. Harris sent us, and he told me to ask for the Harriet. He said you'd know what that meant."

Chapter Twelve

The Dissenters

Harris is dead.

That was the first thing Hanu said out loud in somewhere around two days, and it wasn't even said to another person. He had holed himself up in one of the rooms when they arrived at Deprogramming, and hadn't said a word to anyone since.

The sooner he admitted the reality, the sooner he could get over it. So he told himself firmly, that Harris was dead and there was nothing more to it. It's not like he even knew the man all that well, he reasoned. And maybe Harris was happier now that he was finally with his daughter again. But that didn't make him feel better at all. They were just words.

Hanu sat up in bed. His muscles ached again. They were always aching nowadays. It seemed like once he had recovered, he turned around and had to wear himself out again, running. *What a joke*, he thought. The idea of running, sneaking, fighting to just live your own life your own planet… just didn't make sense.

He wasn't sure how long ago it happened, being as getting here was a lot trickier this time. Everything after he was dragged into the coffeehouse was a dull blur. He remembered being moved to the back office, where Adam did the surgery on Celia and the twins. Hanu couldn't even muster the energy to try and console La as be bawled uncontrollably after drinking the yellow stuff from the vial. He just watched, dazed, as the little boy shook with fear. Celia stroked his dark hair and rocked him.

Adam had called for a ferry, but he said it would take some time before anyone would get there. After a while, Hanu asked that he just let them in the tunnel. 'I've been there before. I'll find my way back, just tell Paula I'm coming with three others,' he said. He didn't really feel like dealing with all of Ellie's jabbering, anyway.

But then they got lost in the tunnel. Hanu thought it would be simple enough to find the main path and take it all the way to Deprogramming, but in this tunnel there were several dummy trails. Some paths just led to the sewer system, and others just led to dead ends. After a while, though, he found the main path that led to the staircase and the luminescent doorway. When Paula opened the door, he pushed past her and went straight to his room.

Hanu had been lying in bed since then, lost in his thoughts. But today he finally got up, tired of the silence. He couldn't stand the loneliness anymore, but he didn't want to have to talk to people either. He looked down the stairs. He could see that Paula had been packing up. Everything from the food pantry was on the table now, and she was putting it in boxes. Celia and the twins must have already gone on to the

Underground. He wondered how Paula tested them before approving them to go. Well, at least they were off to their happy ending, he thought.

Paula saw Hanu and headed up the stairs.

"Can I come in?"

"Sure," Hanu said, sitting back down on his bed. He figured he couldn't keep giving her the cold shoulder after all she'd done for him. She came to his room on several occasions offering food and water, or a change of clothes, but he never once said a word of thanks. She would just set the tray down on his dresser and return to collect the empty dishes later. She'd been patient with him, for sure.

"Who would've thought the dandelion would have the guts to stick it to the Council," she said, smirking.

Angry flames twisted in Hanu's gut. He wouldn't have let her come in if he knew she'd be making jokes. He knew that taking his anger out on Paula wasn't wise, though, so he just sat in silence. Paula came and sat down next to him.

"Celia told me what happened, Hanu. I'm sorry about your friend. He must've been pretty brave to do that for you," she said.

"Can we please talk about something else," Hanu said, looking at her shoes. He was trying his best to be polite, because what happened wasn't Paula's fault. But he didn't want her talking about Harris like she knew him or even cared. It was Hanu's burden to deal with.

"Of course, Hanu," she said quietly. He could tell that Paula was looking at him, but he didn't meet her gaze. He kept looking at her shoes. They were the same ones she always wore- simple black sandals. He wondered if she was testing him, maybe seeing if he was still fit to go to the Underground. He didn't bother to try and convince her, if she was, because he wasn't sure if he even wanted to go anymore. The way he saw it, somebody had to pay for what the scouts did to Harris, and he couldn't make anyone pay if he was hanging out in the Underground.

"You'll be happy to hear that your friends made it," she said, hoping to cheer him up. "Reggie and Andy helped to get them to the Underground. You made a big sacrifice, Hanu. You took a chance to help others, and it paid off. I'm proud of you."

"So they all left without me, huh?" Hanu said sullenly. He was trying to keep his voice from shaking. "They just all took off to the Underground. Not one person tried to come back for me?"

"It wasn't easy for them, Hanu. Reggie was badly injured, and we needed to get those children to the Underground fast. Nobody was in any condition to break back into the District, especially since Andy had just blasted a hole through the wall. The Ancients themselves were crawling through the city looking for us."

"I risked it for them!" Hanu yelled, standing up now. He knew he was being unreasonable, but he couldn't control himself anymore. He crossed the room and swept the dishes off his dresser. "They had me caged up for all that time, and not one person came to help me! Do you have any idea what they did to me in there?"

Chapter Twelve

Paula sat quietly, watching Hanu as he tore the room up. He punched at the stone walls, ignoring the pain in his fists, and screamed through sobs.

"You can't even imagine what it was like! Everyone must've had some real good laughs, huh? I bet they were just kicking back around the camp fire. Did anyone even try? No, they just left me! Forget them!"

He turned around, mid punch, and saw Paula sitting there coolly. She looked just like Mr. Carlisle, back at The Flush. He wanted to punch her right in the old face, to make her feel as much pain he'd felt these last few weeks. Hanu stopped. He knew he was taking it too far. How could he think about hurting Paula? Hanu slumped to the floor, crying.

"Forget them," he sniffled. "Akesh, Reggie, Andy…Harris…my stupid mom… They all left me behind." Paula sat down next to him and stroked his curls. When the sobbing subsided she helped him to his feet.

"Come on, Hanu. Let's get some fresh air."

Downstairs, Hanu sat at the table and watched Paula pack up. She asked him to help, but he just kept dumping the food in boxes haphazardly and staring off into space, so she finally told him to have a seat and relax. She talked to him about different random things, to keep his mind occupied, and Hanu appreciated it even though it didn't work very well. He ended up falling back into his own thoughts for the most part, so she would have to yell at him to pay attention.

"From what I hear, the Council is going nuts," Paula said. "And rightfully so, you guys did quite a number on them.

They lost well over twenty test subjects. Remember what I told you? They need that DNA."

"Yeah one of the ladies there said that humans were mutating faster now- that the Ancients were going to get ahead this time," Hanu said.

"*Mutating*" Paula scoffed. "They sure do have those District personnel under their thumb… Well, you made sure to ruin that for them!"

Paula smiled at Hanu, and he couldn't help but feel a little proud of himself. "What else did they say? Anything of importance?"

"Well, nothing else, really…" Hanu said, thinking. He thought about telling her that his mom was working for them, but he was too ashamed of that. Then he thought about what he had told them. "I do have to admit something though, Paula."

"Hanu I'm sure they did horrible things to you to get you to talk, so don't feel ashamed if you slipped up," she said knowingly. "Besides, you don't really know too much to tell in the first place. And you couldn't have said too much because if they knew our location they would've already come. It must've taken a lot of will power to hold your tongue, Hanu, but it would be helpful to know exactly what was said."

"Well I think it's my fault that they went and tore down the Bathtub Resort and all those other places. That councilman- Aric- was controlling me somehow. It was like… I felt really lazy and tired all of a sudden. Then he asked where my friends were, and I said that they were from regular places in the city." Hanu hung his head. "And they have one of the holographic cloaks, too. They're not safe to use anymore."

Chapter Twelve

"Is that it?"

"Well, yeah… I think so," he said quietly.

"Well that's hardly anything to bat an eye at," she cried, relieved. Paula slapped him on the back and went to grab another box.

"Paula?"

"Yeah, kiddo?" She put the collapsed box on the table and began folding it.

"Are you guys the Dissenters?" he asked. Paula stopped what she was doing and looked at Hanu.

"There's no such thing as the Dissenters, Hanu. They label people Dissenters as a means to an end. It makes it easier to kill whoever threatens their plans."

Hanu had heard that before, but it couldn't explain away what he saw.

"But some people are doing bad things out there. I heard them talking about it at The Flush and then again in the District. They showed me how the Dissenters killed people in an apartment building and destroyed crops and starved people. They're on a religious quest-"

"There's no religious quest, Hanu. I know who did all of those horrible things you saw, and I agree with the actions of those "Dissenters" one hundred percent."

Hanu was taken aback. "They killed people, Paula!"

"Stuff it," she said gruffly. "Someone who lived in that apartment complex was ferrying people to Deprogramming, just like Ellie. When the Ancients came for information the man refused to talk, so they blew him up as well as his family and neighbors. Then they blamed it on Dissenters."

Paula was throwing bags of grain into the box now.

"As for the crops- they regularly produce genetically modified crops that are designed to alter humanity's DNA. Every once in a while someone plucks up the courage to burn them down for us. But don't worry, those people didn't starve because of it. You better believe the Ancients have the power to replicate food with their technology. That's why starvation is literally unheard of nowadays, unless the Ancient Ones decide it's necessary."

"So you mean to tell me…"

Paula walked around the table and leaned in on Hanu. "I mean to tell you that the Ancient Ones will always lie in order to tighten their control. If you want to use that name to group people together, then go ahead. If that's the case, the answer to your question would be yes. We are the Dissenters, and our mission is to fight the Ancients when and how we can! And guess what, Hanu, you're a full-fledged member. You happy now?"

Hanu sank back in his seat. It couldn't just be so simple. But Paula was one of the few people in the world that he would believe because she never minded being frank, no matter how ugly the truth was. He sat and watched as she continued packing the grains into the box.

The Ancient Ones call them Dissenters. He thought about Aric, so desperate to find them. The Ancient Ones must fear them pretty badly to be this cautious. Hanu did prefer to use that name. Paula, Ellie, Toni, Reggie- even Moira and John- they're all Dissenters. They fight the Ancient Ones when and how they can. And he was a Dissenter, too. He let his thoughts roll around in his mind.

"Have you ever killed anyone?" he asked, just to make sure.

"No, but I *have* blown up a building or two to save a friend," she smiled.

Hanu picked up the box she finished packing and put it by the door. He never asked why she was packing all the food away. Maybe she would ship it off to where it was needed more, or maybe since Toni was out of commission she wouldn't have very many people coming through anymore.

"So has business slowed down for you or something?"

"You and I will be the last ones to make the pilgrimage to the Underground from here, Hanu. At least for a little while."

"Well what about the other people on the surface? The ones who are waking up- how will they find the Underground?"

"There are other Deprogramming stations around. I don't think all of them will close down, at least I hope not. But anyways, the people who are meant to find the Underground will get there, one way or another."

Paula closed off the box of dry foods. "Besides, I'll be back one day, when it's safer."

"But Paula, they're going to just keep taking people prisoner if you guys shut down. Everybody up there will be stuck!" Hanu said.

"You did what you could, Hanu, just like I did what I could. Our jobs are done. All we can do is live the best life we can and wait it out," Paula said.

Hanu crossed his arms now, pacing the room. People were going to keep dying. He thought about the Ancient One he saw the day he was caught- the one doing a surgery on that other being. *These things came into a world thinking they can do whatever they want*, he thought to himself, silently fuming. And now what little they were doing about it was about to come to a halt.

Hanu closed his eyes and breathed, trying to control the surging in his gut as he clenched his swollen fists. He was so tired of feeling like this. How could they be born into such a messed up world? How could they be so helpless? It was so unfair. He felt trapped, and he wanted out. He wanted to just rip himself out of his own body so he wouldn't have to continue to feel like this.

"If everyone just realized what was going on, they would fight, too," he said to Paula. "People are evolving faster now. If we just told them the truth, then they would fight back, right?"

"In a perfect world, yes. But the people up there have no desire to hear the truth. Sure, many of them sense that things aren't right on our planet, Hanu, but they're easily consoled by the Ancient Ones and the Council. They're fed with so many lies that the truth makes them uncomfortable, so they brush it off as urban legends and myths- hardly worth considering, let alone acting on."

"But this is different. We're evolving faster now, Paula. Maybe we can get through to enough people!" Hanu argued.

"What, me and you?" Paula laughed as she dropped another box at the tunnel door. "Two people can't make such a difference, Hanu. Besides, we've done enough for now, so please get it out of your head."

Hanu threw a pebble into the water. "Well if you're not going to help, I'll just do it myself."

"What, run Deprogramming?"

Hanu thought about it. Could he take over as the next operator and let Paula move on? She was right, she *had* done her job. Maybe she could just retire. But he was much too young, too inexperienced. He wouldn't last a day. He had to do something, though.

"If I talk to my mom, she might listen. She's a geneticist. She can tell her co-workers the truth! People need to know, and we need to tell them now before they find other people to experiment on."

"You can't do it all on your own, Hanu. Your mom's the one who sent you to the Flush in the first place! Please just come with me to the Underground." Paula walked over to Hanu and grabbed his shoulders. "Haven't you been through enough?"

Hanu's palms started sweating, and his chest was tight. Suddenly he was back in the metal cell, helpless again. He pushed Paula off of him. "You can't control me!"

He backed away from her. "You're right. I've been through enough, but I'm going back. I'm going to tell whoever will listen, Paula. I can't just leave this alone." Hanu continued backing away from her. The corners of his mouth ached from scowling so deeply, but he couldn't control his emotions anymore. “Not after what they did to me... and what they did to Harris,” his voice cracked. “My little sister’s still up there and if she’s like me, my mom will send her off, too. She shouldn’t have to live in a world like this.”

Hanu looked for the tunnel that they came from- the one that leads to the coffeehouse.

“You moron, you’re going to throw away everyone’s sacrifices! Your mom doesn’t know any better. She’ll turn you in.”

“Then she’ll learn better!” Hanu screamed stubbornly, trying to pull the door open. But it was locked. Paula walked over to the keypad.

“So you’ll convince your mom to see reason, then what?”

“Let me out!”

“What will you do?”

Hanu rested his forehead against the door. “I don’t know, Paula. These things have to be stopped, though. I’ll come up with something… I always do.”

“You can’t come back, Hanu. I won’t be here.”

Hanu thought about Akesh and the others in the Underground. He hoped they had found their place in the city and were keeping each other happy. He thought about Reggie and Andy. They must be back in the City of Fire by now. He thought about what Reggie said: “*They do something about it. They can’t help but fight the system.*”

Maybe he should go to the City of Fire and get advice from them. But then again, he knew his plan was a farfetched one; they might try to stop him, too. This was a one man mission, and if he didn't come back, it was because he wasn't alive. Hanu was perfectly fine with that at the moment.

"I didn't plan on it," he said.

Paula shifted her weight, preparing to continue the argument, but thought better of it. She slowly put in the code.

"I know you have to do this, Hanu. Just remember that you'll always have help if you know how to call on it," she said. "Do me a favor and don't get yourself caught. Take care, kiddo."

Hanu looked at Paula. He could see that the old lady had tears in her eyes, but he didn't have time to console her. He had to leave before he lost his nerve. Hanu pulled the door open, and slipped through. He was leaving Deprogramming again.

Chapter Thirteen

Home

Hanu walked through the tunnel now, meandering toward his destination. It wasn't like anyone was waiting on a timely appearance from him, so he decided he might as well save his energy. He didn't even worry about the fact that he brought no food or tools at all. He stopped two or three times to rest, knowing that once he was on the surface he'd probably be running for his life, as usual.

He waited at the tunnel entrance now. Sounds of children squealing came from above, so he knew it was daytime. He thought it was genius that they hid the entrance in plain sight- right under the rocks in the children's play area. The last time he was here he couldn't really appreciate the boldness of it, but now that he had nothing to do but think, he couldn't help but be impressed. Hanu shoved his hands into the cool soil, keeping his hands busy in hopes of giving his mind a rest.

When it was completely silent he emerged from the tunnel and into the coffeehouse yard. The door was heavy, covered in rocks as it was, so it took quite some time to get it open. Once the hole was wide enough, he slowly raised his body out of the ground. Then he admired the brilliance again, as he covered the entrance back with a thick layer of rocks. The play area was enclosed by large, overarching bushes, giving him coverage from all sides of the street. Once he was satisfied, he jumped over the little picket fence and into the cool night. He found the sidewalk and walked away from the school, toward his apartment.

There was a time in his life when Hanu was afraid of walking this path alone. He remembered when he entered the first grade, his mom made him start walking to school by himself and it seemed like such a journey. He remembered worrying about getting lost. There were so many different twists and turns, but by the end of the school year he knew the route by heart. After seven years, though, he was kind of rusty.

It wasn't necessarily that things had changed. The Water Distribution Center was still up ahead and he could see the supply store off in the distance where he was to take a right. It was just hard to remember anything else after that. He had been gone for exactly half his life, so he'd forgotten all the little details that he used to know.

Hanu wandered around his neighborhood now, like a ghost. It didn't even matter that he didn't know where he was going anymore. There wasn't a scout in sight, and nobody else was on the street. It's not like anyone would notice him anyway, he thought. He remembered watching the people on the streets through the window of the Convoy. Nobody really *saw* anyone else.

Hanu found a familiar sight- four apartment buildings in a row. He looked to the third one over. The lights were all out. Maybe it was too late to visit, he thought. He didn't want to draw any attention to himself, so he decided he'd wait until morning. Hanu sat in the shadow of a massive tree and got comfortable for the night. He didn't dare sleep while out in the open like this, so he kept watch.

The building was quiet all night as everyone slept. Hanu thought about his family in there, living life without him. He wondered if Kait still slept with the green unicorn she had as a baby. Many nights he wouldn't go to bed until late because she would demand that he make the thing sing her to sleep. It was a nuisance at the time, but now it was a fond memory.

All Hanu had of his family now was memories, really, because it had been so long since he'd seen them. His mom used to come and visit him at the Flush every weekend, then every other weekend, and then visits dwindled until it was just once every couple months. Eventually she stopped visiting and just sent letters, but even those stopped coming after a while. Hanu was understanding, though. He knew it must've been hard enough for her to work as well as raise a toddler, let alone visit another child hundreds of miles away regularly. But at the same time he barely knew them now, and he was wondering what would make him want to try so hard to save these strangers.

When the sun rose over the trees behind him, he knew it would be time for the children to start walking to school, so he tucked himself further into the brush and watched. One by one, but then in droves, they emerged from the buildings and headed toward Neoma Prep. Hanu knew his mother and sister were awake, and that this would be the perfect opportunity to hide amongst the crowd as he made his way in, but he was just too nervous. He couldn't make himself move just yet.

Soon, the neighborhood was alive with people. He knew that if he waited much longer his family would leave for the day, too. So he straightened himself up and dusted off his corduroys, giving himself a pep talk. But just as he was stepping out from behind the tree he saw his mother emerge from the lobby. She wore the same brown overcoat she always had, and her long hair was pulled back into a bun. She smiled into the sunlight, and strode off down the street. She looked so carefree, he thought. Hadn't she heard about what was going on with her first child? Surely they had come to her, at the very least to lie and say he'd joined with the Dissenters and committed some heinous crime. Surely she knew that the Council was hunting him down. If she were worried at all about Hanu, she hid it well as she walked peacefully into the breeze.

Hanu decided he'd allow her to have a good day at work today; he would save the visit for when she came home. And since she was already leaving, that must mean that Kait already left for school. She passed right by him and he didn't even recognize her.

He waited until his mom had completely gone before moving into the building. Then he walked through the lobby, hoping nobody would recognize him. It was unattended.

Perfect.

Hanu climbed the stairs to the second floor, and with each step, he grew more anxious. He realized he was clenching his jaw- he'd been doing a lot of that lately- so he shook himself, trying to relax. When he got to the second floor, he found the door that read 817. Would the code still be the same? He punched it in: 031985.

Click.

Hanu stood for a while with his hand on the doorknob. It was strange to be here. He felt like an intruder. But it's my home, too, he told himself. He pushed the door open. But then he was suddenly nervous.

"Kait?"

He realized his sister could still be home, and it wouldn't do well if he just barged in on her like this.

Nothing.

He stepped in and closed the door behind him. Their apartment changed so much in seven years. They still had the same red couches, but there were new throw pillows. There was also a new kitchen table. And more pictures on the walls, too. He saw a two year old Kait, and a six year old Kait. In one of the pictures she posed in a ballerina's leotard and sunglasses. He smiled, remembering being silly with her when she was just a baby. He thought about what kind of personality she had now. And his mother as well- he wondered how they might have changed in all this time. As he looked at the pictures he started feeling something else, too. There were so many pictures, and he wasn't in very many of them. They looked so happy. Maybe they had moved on without him.

He went into his bedroom. It was exactly how he remembered it- from the stuffed animals on his shelves to the solar system night light he had hanging from the ceiling fan.

Chapter Thirteen

He sat on his bed, sending a cloud of dust into the air. She didn't even bother cleaning his room every once in a while. Hanu tried to keep his feelings in check, but it was getting harder.

He thought better of it, being as he was already upset, but he went into Kait's room anyway. She had a four poster bed now, with pink lace draped across the top in a canopy. She also had a vanity mirror on her wall and little knickknacks adorned her dresser here and there. She was like a princess. Hanu was clenching his fists again as his chest got heavy. He tried to reason with himself that Kait had just grown up and he'd been away. But as much as he wanted to be rational, he couldn't help but feel abandoned.

Hanu closed her door and went back to the living room. He figured there was nothing he could do but wait for them to return. He had come this far, so there was no point in overreacting before he even had a chance to speak his peace.

Hanu laid on the couch, deciding what he would do with himself after he spoke with his mom. Well, it largely depended on how the talk goes, he reasoned. What if he told her everything and she brushed it off as legends and myths, as Paula said? What would he do? Now that he was a little calmer, he realized that he'd put himself in a really bad position. With a sudden twinge in his gut, he thought about the fact that there was absolutely nobody else he could go to for help. Toni was out of the question and Harris was gone.

Of course he could always just go back through the tunnel to Deprogramming and try to find his way to the Underground himself. That was probably his best bet if things turned for the worse here. And what if things turned out for the best, he thought. He didn't even know what he was trying to accomplish, so he wasn't sure what the best would even look like. Would his mother realize that he was right and commit to joining him in spreading truth? Would she hide him at home while she went to work, or better, agree to become the new ferry or operator of Deprogramming? Now that he was actually here, he realized how childish he was being. But he had to try. If there was the slightest chance he could save his family from this farce, he would try.

Hanu dozed on the couch. He wouldn't allow himself to fall asleep completely, but he laid back and tried to relax his mind. He'd been thinking so much for the last few days that it felt like he would catch a brain cramp. He thought about the illustration of the brain in the Tome of the Earth. He wondered if humans could actually get cramps in their brains, but the Tome never mentioned it. Then he thought about the strand of DNA and the picture of the other races. He thought about the creature with the whiskers- *Galedeus*.

"Why don't you help me!" he heard his own voice. Then he sat up, startled. He forgot he was on his couch at home.

Hanu decided he'd keep his mind occupied with something constructive. He reached over and grabbed a book from the coffee table to read. It was a dictionary. He figured that since he had some time to kill he'd just learn some new words. He opened the book to a random page and pointed: Gallant, adjective, 1. (of a person or behavior) brave or heroic. He knew that one already. He flipped again and pointed: Meticulous, adjective, 1. showing great attention to detail; very careful and precise. That's a new one. Hanu thought about how he might use the word in the near future. Then he thought about a word he'd been meaning to find the definition for. He flipped back and ran his finger down the page until he found it: Martyr, noun, 1. a person who is killed because of their religion or beliefs. Verb 1. kill (someone) because of their beliefs.

Hanu thought back to his dream. He tried to remember the exact words, so that he could put it all in context with the meaning he now had. And besides…I don't want to become a martyr, he had said.

Hanu laughed. *Well, a lot had changed since that dream*, he thought. Nowadays, he pretty much had been avoiding death at every turn because of his beliefs. He supposed he was a martyr, or at least well on his way to becoming one. But Hanu didn't *really* want to die, even though he may have been careless lately.

He put the book down and went to the kitchen for some food. He wouldn't think about that. He would just focus on staying alive for his beliefs for now.

Hanu was sitting at the kitchen table when his family came home. The girls clamored through the door and chattered happily as they took their shoes off. Then Kara stopped midway through taking off her overcoat.

"Hi, mom."

Hanu wasn't sure of what to say when she got there. He thought about just starting off strong and letting it all out as soon as she walked in, but he didn't want to seem like he actually was crazy, so he figured he'd keep it simple. She stood in the doorway, staring into the kitchen, unbelieving. Kait hid behind her.

“It’s me, Hanu.” He felt a little insulted that his sister would hide from him. Had his mom told her that he was just some reckless psychopath?

“I know my baby when I see him,” she whispered.

“I’m sorry to just drop in like this. I’m sure you heard that some things have been going on with me,” he said, standing up now.

“No it’s just fine.” She walked into the kitchen, arms outstretched. “Look at you!”

He hugged her tightly, letting tears fall on her neck. Kait stood at the door, unsure of what to do.

“Let me just use the bathroom, baby. I’ve been holding it all day,” she said, smiling through tears. Then she left Hanu alone with Kait, still in the doorway.

“So you’re in the third grade by now, huh?” he said, trying to make small talk. He wanted to sound as normal as he could, so as not to scare her.

“Second.” She didn’t seem to want to talk to him, which made him more upset.

“Don’t you remember me, Kait? You used to sleep in my bed with me and I would make your green unicorn sing to you and…” Hanu stopped talking. He knew he must’ve sounded like a crazy person now. She was looking confused.

Chapter Thirteen

"I've been away, Kait, but I'm still the same old me," he said. Kait stood in the doorway, quietly watching Hanu struggle at the table.

"Come on, Kait, and sit down with us," his mom said. She had come back from the bathroom and was pulling up a couple of chairs for them.

"Now tell me, what's going on with you?" she asked. Her face twisted into a concerned scowl.

Hanu didn't know where to begin. Now that she was here his mouth was incredibly dry. He had so much to say before, but now he couldn't even think of a single thing. But he was here now, and this is what he'd been waiting on, so he opened up his mouth.

"Mom, I know you're a geneticist and you've been to the district to work on children."

"Okay, but what does that have to do with what's been happening with *you,* Hanu? I've heard all these crazy things- that you've destroyed a Convoy and ran away. People were hurt. Tell me you have an explanation."

"Well that did happen, but it wasn't me. I was there, but... it just happened, mom. They were taking us in for override!" Hanu stood up. This wasn't going as planned. He didn't imagine she would just jump down his throat like this before he even had a chance to talk. He paced the kitchen now, glancing out the window.

"Mom, I need you to listen. There's something important I have to tell you. These people- the Council- they're just using us. They take the kids from the Flush to do these experiments, mom."

"I know that, Hanu! That's part of the job description. We work to help children like you. You should've just gone in for testing!"

"No, mom. You haven't seen the conditions they keep us in. You don't know what they did to me, mom. They're torturing kids in there!"

Hanu was furious now. He stopped pacing and crossed his arms, looking at his mom. She wasn't even trying to hear him out. He looked at Kait, who was watching him with sorrowful eyes. He didn't want her to think he was crazy, to feel sorry for him.

"Mom, they're acting on the orders of the Ancients, but the Ancient Ones aren't who they say they are. They've been lying to us. When I was in the District, one of them told me that they lie to other races from space in order to steal what they want from them. He admitted it to me, mom!"

"Hanu, there are no other races in space. We're the only ones, baby. The Ancient Ones created us, and us alone. Whatever they're doing, we have to trust in their wisdom because they know things that we don't."

"You're right. They know a lot of things we don't, mom. They know that humans are evolving and if they let us evolve naturally they won't be able to lie to us anymore. We'll be able to see the truth for ourselves," he said. Hanu was feeling more confident now that he had gotten into a flow. "And there are other races out there- a whole bunch of them! I've seen them in the District, too."

Chapter Thirteen

There was an abrupt knock on the door, making Hanu jump. Kara stood up now, too, and walked over to the door.

"Baby, you're sick, and the Dissenters brainwashed you. I called the scouts to come get you. Please go with them and get your tests done."

Hanu didn't plan on this. He thought at the very least, that he would just storm off after she decided not to hear him out. Now he didn't even have that luxury. Without even thinking, he darted to his room. He heard his mom yell something down the hall, but it was undistinguishable. Maybe she thought he would just jump in his bed and refuse to go. Well, at least he could take advantage of her ignorance.

He would sneak out of his window and hide in the shadows between the two buildings, then be off before the scouts even entered his room. He unlocked the window and tried to lower himself down gently, but he fell, banging his head on the sidewalk.

Hanu tried to pick himself up. Now wasn't the time to lose his senses. He rolled over onto his knees and tried to stand, but he couldn't make out what he was looking at. Dizzy, he tried to at least move himself into the bushes. Thoughts were flashing in his mind now, as he tried to remember why he was running. He thought about rolling around in the Convoy as it crashed onto the sidewalk, then he thought about Aric punching him to the ground.

"Why… don't… you…" he stammered. "Why…"

Hanu pricked himself on the bush he was crawling into. "Why don't you… help me?" He grabbed at the bush, remembering now that he was outside of his house, and that scouts were coming to take him back to the District- or worse, to kill him.

He looked around now, blinking hard. They hadn't come out yet, so maybe there was still time to put distance between himself and the scouts. He shuffled down the sidewalk. Darkness was falling, and he would soon have the advantage. He looked for his trademark escape route- an alley.

"Again!" he yelled to nobody. He was running again. Always running. It's always me, he thought to himself.

"Why don't you help me?" he shouted into the setting sun as he ran through the neighborhood. He thought about what Paula said: *'You'll always have help if you know how to call on it.'*

But no help was coming and he knew it. He ducked into the nearest alley, but before he could even think about his next move a scout had entered through the other side and was running at him full speed. His face was as charming as ever, but Hanu knew what he was capable of. What they did to Harris… he wanted to break that stupid face of his for it.

He sprinted toward the scout now. This would be the last time that the Council would make him run, and he would make it count. He growled as he came for the scouts face.

"I'll be a martyr today!"

Chapter Fourteen

The Other Council

But he never got there. All of a sudden he found himself in a softly lit room. He was caught. Hanu froze, waiting for his senses to detect any type of movement. He was caught off guard, but he was still willing to fight to the death. It was strange, really, that he found himself here suddenly. Had he been knocked out and brought here? No, he was pretty sure that wasn't the case. Besides, his heart was still racing. He was in that alley only seconds ago. And where was here, anyway? He didn't recognize it. Hanu turned, inspecting the place. It was just a room, with brown spongy walls and a large window.

Hanu ran his hand over the soft wall. There didn't seem to be a door to escape through. He crossed over to the window, and his stomach dropped. He could see that Earth was some distance away from wherever he was. This wasn't just any room, he was in a room aboard a spacecraft.

He didn't understand. Had the Ancients grown impatient with the Council and just picked him up themselves? That was a possibility, but if it were that easy why wouldn't they do that sooner? Plus, Hanu didn't feel like this was the work of an Ancient One. This place felt different than what he in felt the district- lighter, somehow.

"You won't be a martyr today," a voice said behind him. Hanu jumped.

He turned around to see a rather short creature with a wrinkled face and whiskers, and wearing maroon robes… *Galedeus*?

"No. Galedeus is, in your understanding, far away," said the creature.

Hanu shook his head, confused. Was this another one of the Council's tricks? Surely they didn't expect him to believe this. They were in his head, somehow.

"I assure you, this is not trickery, Hanu."

"Are you listening to my thoughts?"

"More like feeling your thoughts, but for all intents and purposes, yes. If you choose to feel what I am thinking, then I implore you to do so. I know you're quite adept at it by now."

"Who are you? I want to talk to Galedeus. He's the Ambassador, right?" Hanu said, rather rudely. But he didn't mean to, he had started to panic and Galedeus was a name he knew and trusted.

"You've had no trouble consulting with me before, Hanu. Why do you demand Galedeus now?"

"You… *you're* in my dreams?"

"I am. You know me by Yaar," the old creature smiled.

Hanu thought about what Paula said- about traveling to seek advice from beings in your dreams, but he knew he hadn't fallen asleep. The Tome had described it, too- traveling in an astral body. He grabbed his own arm to make sure he was still in his regular body, not that he would know the difference between the two.

"You are not the one traveling in astral form, Hanu. I am," he said, crossing the room now to get a closer look at him.

"I'm sorry, but who exactly are you? I mean, how do you know me? Or why do you talk to me in my dreams?"

"You've been in our care for a few thousand years, Hanu. We Nergal are your council."

Hanu tried to make himself think. Maybe time for them was different than it was for him. Or maybe they counted it differently. He was quite sure he was only fourteen years old. But that wasn't the most pressing concern right now. Hanu didn't want to ask, because he didn't want to have to sort any more factors into his already miserable life. He was thinking about the Council on Earth, and if these guys were anything like them, he might as well be dropped off at the nearest bush.

"What kind of council, exactly, are you?" he asked.

"We are your Council of Lives. We guide you through your journeys into the lower dimensions. I believe on Earth we have been called guiding spirits or guardian angels, and other things of the sort. Of course, the Ancients would never acknowledge our existence, so there's no name for us now, really," Yaar explained conversationally.

"And do you help everyone else, too?"

"No, just you and a few others," said Yaar, smiling. "There are thousands of other councils serving Earth at this time, though."

Thousands of others? Hanu couldn't believe what he was hearing. All of those councils supposedly helping Earth, and nobody was showing up to give some actual help. But Yaar *did* show up.

"So you *can* interfere?"

"Well, to a certain degree," he admitted, looking rather guilty.

"A certain degree is better than nothing at all!" Hanu exclaimed.

He was becoming rather irritable, though he wasn't sure why he was about to take it out on Yaar. "I mean, you guys are just out there, watching all of this happen? All these other beings out there- can they come here like this, too? For thousands of years, these Ancient Ones, or whoever they really are, have been trying to steal Earth from us, and nobody comes to help?"

And Hanu had to move his body around again. He wrung his shaking hands, trying not to punch at the soft walls. As mad as he was, he didn't want to be thrown off the ship just yet. Not without answers. But somebody had to know how hard it was. And maybe if he told Yaar how bad it had gotten, then he would help.

"This is a necessary struggle, Hanu," Yaar said, but it wasn't what Hanu wanted to hear.

"What do you mean, necessary?" he barked. It's necessary for them to come and take advantage of us like this? For them to lie to us and poison us? How do we fight that? We're just humans!"

The creature beckoned Hanu to the window. They were traveling back toward Earth now, though he didn't feel the ship moving at all. It was as though the window were merely playing a movie. It was a little unsettling.

They skimmed over the city for a few moments, and then moved into a department store. A woman was walking a family into the dressing rooms. Hanu wasn't sure why they were intruding on these people. He was about to turn away when Yaar grabbed him by the arm. The woman began the surgery on the man, and then his wife. As the woman grabbed a black box and pulled out a vial of yellow liquid, they left and returned to the sky.

Then after a few wavering moments they burrowed straight into the ground. They were in a tunnel. Six people walked by, some smiling and others crying. Hanu could feel the elation coming from the group. His throat burned, tangled into a knot; he wanted to cry.

"You're not *just* humans," Yaar explained. "You're resilient. And you're organized. Don't write yourselves off yet. Humanity will overcome."

"But they're more organized. They control everything. And besides, we shouldn't even have to do this."

The old creature met Hanu's eyes with a sure gaze. "Without darkness there is no light, and if there is no light then darkness cannot be spawned."

"What does that even mean?" Hanu said, thoroughly befuddled. The little man laughed.

"Once, long ago, a creature spawned from the great void. It was perfect in every way- it was just and meek and happy. But over the eons it became lonely. It existed in all of its perfection for so long that it forgot who or what it was. It was numb, lacking. One day, from the perfect being sprung another. It was also perfect in every way, but it was the exact opposite of the creature from which it sprang. And so the two locked in an eternal struggle. Through the struggle, the first creature remembered who it was and all of its perfection, and the second creature also realized *its* own perfection."

"I still don't get it," Hanu said. He was really trying to apply the story to Earth's situation, but he couldn't figure out who was supposed to be the first perfect creature and if the second perfect creature could even be perfect if it was opposite of the first one. This kind of inferencing was way more than what the teachers at the Flush prepared him for. And, of course, Yaar already knew this, but he went on just for the sake of telling the story.

"I am saying that without evil, good loses its integrity," he explained. "Your destiny is to struggle against the Ancient Ones to win your planet back. And when it is over, your race will have harvested a deep identity and value for all that it is fighting for, having struggled to earn it."

Hanu let the tears he'd been fighting escape down his cheeks. "How do you know?" he whispered.

"Well, that is the nature of life- or at least one dimension of it. One cannot simply sum up the meaning of life in a single evening." Yaar smiled at Hanu for a moment. "Nothing is set in stone, but I've seen various bright futures for this world. I'm afraid I can't tell you much more, though. I don't want to interfere with your destiny."

Yaar looked out of the window, too. They left the tunnel and had been floating aimlessly above the city. Most of the people were home now, and the lights from their apartment windows dotted the night.

"So why did you help me if you're not supposed to interfere?" Hanu finally asked.

"Well, it was a stretch," Yaar said. "But since you helped some of the intergalactic citizens that were being held prisoner on Earth, I figured this is afforded as an equal reaction in the exchange."

Hanu remembered when they broke Akesh and the others out of the holding facility. He didn't care at the time, but those beings *were* vanishing into thin air. They were returning home.

"They were kept in electromagnetic fields, unable to escape this dimension until you and your friends freed them," Yaar clarified. Hanu glanced over at the small being, who continued looking out of the window. He still wasn't used to Yaar reading his thoughts.

Hanu tried to pinpoint his home- to see if the scouts had gone by now. He wondered how they reacted when he vanished all of a sudden, or if they would be in trouble for returning to the District without him. *Serves them right*, he thought.

"So, since you're here, can you tell me something?" he asked.

"We've been known to offer advice and knowledge from time to time," Yaar said, mocking coy. He knew that Hanu was thinking about Paula's words.

"Who are they, and how are we supposed to fight them, Yaar?"

The creature bent to touch the floor, then he pulled a chair up from it. The floor, which was a very smooth, black material stretched upward and formed perfectly into a very comfortable looking seat. Hanu watched in amazement as he did it again, pulling up a second chair. Then Yaar extended a short arm, inviting Hanu to sit.

"What do you know about dimensions?" he started.

"Well, I know that they are different worlds that are next to each other, and that you can travel from one to another," Hanu said, sitting across from Yaar.

"Very well," Yaar said, nodding his head and relaxing into his seat. "Think about it more as one reality. Certainly you know that the human can see only a small spectrum of light and hear but a limited range of sound, correct?"

"Yeah, I read that in the Tome."

Yaar studied Hanu with quiet eyes before continuing. "Well the other dimensions lie in the spectrum that you cannot detect with your senses, and you ought not if you're not genetically written for them. There are higher dimensions, and lower ones and these are all filled with flora and fauna and beings unfathomable."

"The Ancient Ones had a planet of their own, which was actually very similar to yours, actually. Their destiny was to cultivate spiritual and emotional values, but they failed, and when the time came for their planet to ascend to a higher dimension, they were afraid. They were only able to see on a physical level, having not awakened their spiritual eyes, so the destination of their planet appeared to be a giant black hole."

"They, being highly technologically advanced, created an escape plan. They would colonize another planet, far away from the black hole. When they reached the cusp of the black hole the Ancient Ones, unable to find a compatible planet in time, boarded their ships and escaped into space. Planet less, they began to devolve. Over time they fell into lower dimensions. But from those lower dimensions they continued to search for a planet to steal, so they courted and coerced Earth."

"So what was the black hole?" Hanu asked.

"It is the place that all planets eventually travel through to metamorphose."

Yaar sensed that Hanu was sorting all of the information out as best as he could, so he paused. Hanu opened his mouth, preparing to ask another question, but he wasn't sure of what he wanted to ask. He sat on the edge of his seat, mouth hanging open.

"So we have find the lower dimension that they're coming from?" His face was furrowed from thinking.

"You need not travel there, Hanu. I would like to make a suggestion, if you would hear it."

"Of course," Hanu said. He leaned in closer to Yaar, almost right on top of him now.

"The holes that are torn in this dimension by the nuclear bombs remain open for several hundred years. These portals feed the Ancient Ones, so to say. Their race's life energy pulses through them from the other side, allowing them to continue manifesting here on Earth. Once the portals start to close, they must slip back into the lower dimension. My suggestion is that you close the portals, sending them back. From there humanity can work freely toward fortifying itself against their mental influences."

Hanu groaned. Closing portals sounded no more achievable than jumping to a lower dimension to do battle. Then he remembered his dream when they were discussing his life.

"Will I die?" he asked. "You know, become a martyr?"

"When you came to Earth this time around- and yes you've been here before- you chose to become fully awakened," Yaar said. "Some people decide to never detect a thing and live happily on Earth, but you couldn't do it anymore. You decided you would rather die fighting for your convictions- to change the world."

Hanu thought about it. This is exactly what his choices have led him to, so he really shouldn't have been surprised. He couldn't just go to the Underground like everyone else.

"So I *will* die?"

He may have acted recklessly, but now that Hanu had confirmed the conversations he'd had about being a martyr were real, he decided he didn't really *want* to die. He was too young.

"The future is not certain. And this task doesn't have to be your final one, no," Yaar said. "I think you'll find that it is rather achievable, for you already have the information and tools you need."

"What do you mean?" Hanu sat back up in his seat.

Yaar gestured for Hanu to look through the window again. From his seat, he could see that they were on the move. They were traveling through the scarred parts of the land now. Hanu could see that off in the distance, the ground was glowing as if it had caught the day's sunlight and was releasing it into the darkness. They approached the glowing part of the Earth and plunged downward. When he could see again, Hanu realized that they were in an enormous city.

There were buildings of all shapes and sizes, and rolling pastures dotted with bulky animals. Some of the roads were cobbled and others were wide dirt roads. There were lakes and flowing rivers, and flying things in the air. Hanu looked up to where they just came from, but he could only see a dark sky speckled with clouds and a watchful moon. The stars winked at him as if to acknowledge his presence.

Hanu got up and pressed his face into the window. "This is the Underground," he said in awe.

Hanu always imagined the Underground to be a dusty little hole in the ground where everyone huddled together for warmth, but this place was the exact opposite. It was open and free.

"It is."

Yaar stood up too, and they watched the Underground sleep for a while.

"So are the tools and information here, then?" Hanu asked.

"Well, yes. You must understand that the people living in the Underground are evolving toward the fourth dimension. They are opening up the fourth dimensional reality here on Earth."

"Yeah, Paula told us that."

"Well, the energy that is emanating from here acts as a deterrent. The Ancient Ones cannot detect the hidden cities here because they cannot fathom their existence, but they are slightly aware of the energy. They believe these areas to be dangerous and uncharted territory, and would rather not meddle." Yaar chuckled. "And rightfully so- the energy here transmutes their own. This energy is also what closes those portals."

Hanu thought about what that meant. Would he have to move the entire city next to the portals? Could he get the Underground to do that- just travel around closing them? But he doesn't even know where these portals are, or even how *many* of them there are, for that matter, he thought.

"Six, currently. And you should be able to guess where they might be located."

"What?" Hanu said, trying to figure out what Yaar was talking about, until he remembered that he could hear his thoughts. "Oh, well if I had to guess… um..."

"These portals are quite large, mind you," said Yaar.

"Well they're big, and I guess the Ancient Ones would be near them because of the life energy thing..."

"Go on…"

"The District of Operations- of course!" Hanu exclaimed.

Yaar smiled delightedly. "Yes there's one at the District here on this continent. I was beginning to think I'd have to spoon feed you the entire thing! You know, I'm really toeing the line by helping you this much, Hanu."

Hanu wanted to grab up the little man into a hug, but he wasn't sure if that was appropriate or not. "I really appreciate you coming, Yaar," he said smiling congenially. It was his first heartfelt smile in what seemed like ages.

Yaar looked at Hanu as if debating with himself about something. Then he reluctantly spoke. "I don't suppose that since I'm here, and you were a big help to those other citizens… Well it's rightfully yours, anyway…It's just leveling the playing field… "

Hanu watched as Yaar talked it over with himself.

"I don't think it would be unfitting if I left you with a parting gift, Hanu," he finally said.

"Okay, well, what is it?" Hanu tried to sound nonchalant. He hardly ever received gifts, and eagerly wondered what one might receive from a member of his Council of Lives.

"Well, it's really a gradual process, but being as you would've already had it if it weren't for the Ancient Ones interfering, I'd like to attune your cells to the fourth dimension."

And it was Hanu's turn to be reluctant. "Well what does that do?" he asked.

"Well, fourth dimensional energy is your birthright. And remember what I said about the fourth dimensional energies here at the Underground," Yaar explained excitedly.

Hanu thought about the possibilities. Would he be able to close the portals if the Underground didn't want to help? That was enough to convince him, in and of itself.

"I accept," he said, puffing his chest out.

"Very well."

Hanu could tell from looking through the window that they had already ascended toward the sky. They were returning above ground. He looked around anxiously, thinking that maybe some tools would appear out of nowhere. He wasn't exactly sure how people were attuned, and now that he was thinking about it, he probably should have asked before accepting. He wondered if it would be anything like the vial of lemon that he'd had at the Bathtub Resort. He looked to Yaar, knowing that he was listening in.

"I think you'll find that it's much more enjoyable," he assured Hanu. Hanu nodded his head, relieved. "Okay, so what do I have to do?"

"Nothing at all, except stand or sit, whichever would make you more comfortable. I will do the work- when you're ready. Just know, Hanu, I cannot interfere again after this."

Hanu sat, but then he stood up again. He was getting a little anxious, not knowing what would be happening soon.

Then he sat back down again. "Just go ahead, Yaar. I'm as ready as I can be."

Yaar pulled back his robes, revealing hands with three amphibious fingers each. His palms were glowing now, with the same energy Hanu saw coming from the ground. He placed it over Hanu's forehead. Then Hanu could feel his voice.

"Hon sha ze sho nen. Cho ku rei. Sei he ki."

Hanu felt a warmth spreading from the top of his head, as if someone was pouring a liquid over him. It started at the very top and emanated downward.

"*Dai Ko Myo. Raku."*

Chapter Fifteen

Hanu's Resolve

Hanu became less aware of Yaar's words, if he was still speaking, and more aware of his own heartbeat. He closed his eyes and listened. Sure and strong, it beat on, and everything else fell away.

After a few rhythmic moments the heartbeat began to slow, and Hanu was afraid it would stop. He tried to will it to keep beating, but he found that the more he struggled, the slower it beat. He silently panicked, urging his heart not to give in, and then he realized that it was inevitable.

Hanu forfeit his life. He figured that if this would kill him, he would go peacefully. He was tired of being fearful, and honestly no longer saw the benefit of it. He was finished with running and hiding, and he was tired of his heart constantly racing.

But he didn't die. Suddenly he was aware that he could sense everything around him. Though his eyes were closed, he could tell he was in a spacecraft, but it wasn't a spacecraft. He realized that it was *alive.* This vehicle was Yaar's astral body.

It was what enabled Yaar to be here with Hanu in this dimension.

He also sensed the Earth below. The sphere was more than a large chunk of dirt and rock- it was also alive. He could feel that she was struggling, that certain places on the planet were decaying, but her pulse was strong. He felt he could go and speak with the planet as if she were one giant being.

He detected that the air itself was thick with energy. He could see it spiraling in the air in certain places. In other places he could see this energy take on the form of wildlife. This is what Vanessa had been seeing the whole time. He, on occasion, would catch glimpses of these things, but never as he saw them now.

Hanu pulled a deep breath in, and felt life pulsing through him. Then he exhaled, and as he did he felt that he had slipped into nothingness. Into a void. But he wasn't afraid, because he knew that in the next breath he could be whatever he chose. He *was* potential.

ᘓᘓᘓᘓᘓᘓᘓ

After a few moments, or possibly an eternity, Hanu came to. And when he did, he found that he was sitting on a bench at Tantra Coffeehouse. He looked around, perplexed. Children were playing in the rocks as parents congregated at the various tables in the yard. It seemed as though nobody noticed that a boy had suddenly appeared out of nowhere.

Hanu looked at his hands. He was shaking so hard that he wouldn't have been surprised if they were blurred. Hanu took a deep breath in and ran his hands through his curls. Whatever Yaar had done to him, it seemed it would take some time to get comfortable in his own skin again. Hanu leaned back in the seat.

Had Yaar meant for him to head back to the Underground through this route? Hanu knew he would have to deliver the information soon. He couldn't do it alone. Maybe he should've told him that Paula no longer operated Deprogramming down there.

Hanu sighed. He was just in the Underground with Yaar, and now he had to find his way back. *Well, maybe getting back is all part of the struggle*, he thought. Or maybe Yaar intended for Hanu to choose for himself what he would do next. He *did* say that he wouldn't be interfering anymore.

Whatever the reason, though, Hanu realized that this was a good place to be right now. There was something he had to do.

The sun, rising in the east, told Hanu that it should be around midmorning. He stood up and oriented himself, then he stepped over the picket fence and walked off. Hanu was no longer afraid of walking out in the open. His meeting with Yaar had incited a confidence that Hanu never felt before. He knew their secret, and he would soon be using it against the Ancient Ones. He crossed the street and headed toward the park space, almost daring someone to approach him.

While he walked, Hanu thought about his journey over these last few weeks. He had escaped the District of Operations twice now, and saw his family for the first time in years. Then he tried to attack a scout, and was taken aboard a living craft to speak with an other-worldly being who gave him a gift. If someone had told him a month ago that all of this would be happening, he would've thought *them* crazy.

Midway down the street, Hanu stopped in his tracks. Just around the corner somewhere, something else had happened recently. He didn't dare look directly down the alley, but allowed himself to peek from his periphery. Maybe Harris hadn't died that day, but was just beat up badly, and was waiting for Hanu to return to save him. But Hanu knew that wasn't possible. He knew what he saw that day.

Hanu wondered why Yaar didn't intervene then. Well, maybe because he wasn't a part Harris' council, he reasoned. He wondered what Harris' council was like, and if they thought about intervening. Maybe they allowed him to die because it was part of Harris' struggle.

A month ago, Hanu wouldn't have believed that he'd meet someone that would change his life so drastically, and that he would be gone in an instant. But it did happen, and despite that and all the other terrible things that the Ancient Ones had done to him, it seemed as though destiny was on his side.

Hanu continued walking a little more quickly now. Then he realized something: Harris died for what he believed in. He was also a martyr. And in this way, Hanu felt more connected to the man.

He knew he was taking another risk by coming here, but he had to do this first. After all, he would have to make it to the Underground without Paula's help and then try to convince them to fight. Hanu didn't even know the mechanics of closing a portal, so he would have to hope that someone else had that information. The task he had to try and carry out would probably kill him, regardless of what Yaar said, so he needed to speak his peace while he could.

Hanu walked past a blue door now. He knew he was on the right route. He would go just a little further and cut into the building with the statue in front.

When Hanu walked into the lobby of the apartments the clerk gave him a nod. Hanu thought for a moment that maybe he had recognized him, but he was just being friendly. Hanu waved back, then he took the stairs for privacy. When he got to the fourth floor he checked Harris' doorknob. He knew that he locked it the last time they left, but he checked anyway. Hanu stood at the locked door, trying to figure out how he'd get in. He checked the little window beside the door. It was also locked.

He silently apologized to Harris and shoved his fist through the middle of the window. Glass fell to the floor as it shattered. Hanu looked around. Nobody noticed. He quickly unlocked the window and pulled it open, then he leaned into the apartment and unlocked the door.

Hanu walked in slowly, and took in the now familiar smell of oregano. All of Harris' books were thrown to the floor and plaster was knocked off of the walls in some places. He thought about the Ancient Ones blowing up that other building. *Guess they didn't have to blow Harris' place up; they already killed his only family*, he thought. But they did destroy the man's belongings. Hanu felt his nostrils flare as he looked on in disbelief. But it didn't matter because Hanu planned on destroying *their* belongings, too. This just added fuel to his fire.

Chapter Fifteen

Hanu picked up a couch cushion. It looked like they were searching for something. Maybe they confiscated some of his things, he thought. Hanu tearfully looked under the coffee table and found his rock collection. He slid the box out and opened it. The gemstones and rocks had kept their secret. Hanu collected four shiny black pyramids and three rocks, and put them in his pocket. He might need them later.

"They messed your place up pretty bad, Harris," he said quietly. "I'm sorry."

Then he picked up Harris' books and carefully replaced them on the shelves. He smoothed out the wrinkled pages and put them back into their neat rows like they were before. Then he went to the kitchen and did as Harris had done so many times- he packed a bag of food and found a spare change of clothing.

He went into the bathroom and washed up. His face was scratched from the bushes and he looked much older, *worn*. Hanu looked in the cabinet for a pair of scissors. He found a heavy silver pair, for cutting hair. Perfect. He leaned over the countertop, grabbing a lock of his own curls, and he started clipping.

"You're not a kid anymore, Hanu," he told himself rather proudly. And he smoothed out what was left of his hair.

When he was finished, he went back to the living room. It was mostly cleaned, besides the big holes in the walls. He sat at the table and ate some bread and jelly that he found in the refrigerator, and as he did he thought about Harris' daughter. He wondered if Harris would have still chosen to lead people to the Underground if she was alive.

He stood up, noticing the plants under the window. Nobody had come to give them water or open the blinds for them, and they were dying. Hanu knew he couldn't stay here for much longer, and neither could they. They would surely die. So he quickly pulled the door open and checked the hall. Then he grabbed the first pot and carried it to the elevator. He pushed the button with the R on it. When the door opened, he carried the pot onto the roof and put it up against a cement shaft. Here, it would get plenty of sun.

He did the same for six other pots, rescuing them all in turn, and on the last trip he brought a big blue watering can. When we was finished watering the last one he sat on the cement shaft. The curt breeze felt strange against Hanu's head- it was no longer protected by his curls.

He looked over the city. The roofs of the apartment complexes were separated by treetops and supply stores here and there. Further off were the oddly shaped buildings in the Entertainment District, and then the modest skyscrapers off in the Business District. Hanu trained his gaze further into the city until he finally set his steeled eyes on those massive walls looming in the distance.

"Why can't we just be free, Harris?" he whispered into the wind.

There had been so much that he wanted to say to Harris and never got the chance, so he let it out now, hoping that the words would reach him.

"I'm sorry your daughter died, and I hope that you found her. I know she would be happy to see you," he said gently. "I didn't know you very well, but I feel like you could have been like a father to me, you know, if we went to the Underground when we had the chance."

That lump came back to Hanu's throat, warning him. He couldn't let the words out all at once or their heaviness would crush him, suffocate him. He would have to set them free little by little so that the wind could carry them to wherever Harris was. Hanu paused for a while, wiping his face with his two-sizes-too-big shirt. Then he looked up, letting the sun warm him.

"I actually went to see my mom and my sister. They still think I'm crazy," he said, laughing now. "But it doesn't matter. I'm going to save them anyway, Harris."

Hanu stood up and walked to the edge of the roof. Looking at the District walls in the distance, he exhaled, knowing that in the next breath he would decide his future.

"I'm a full-fledged Dissenter now," Hanu smiled to himself proudly, thinking about Paula's words. "I'm going to fight the Ancient Ones when and how I can. There's a portal in there and we're going to close it, Harris. I'm going to find Reggie and Andy and that's the first thing we'll do. After that, we'll go after the rest of them and wake our planet up."

About the Author

Sasha DeVore lives a peaceful life in the Underground of Manor, TX with her husband, son and two dogs. She enjoys writing YA Fiction, Adventure and Fantasy.

The Adventure has just begun!

Read the second book in the Wake Trilogy

What will happen next?

CPSIA information can be obtained
at www.ICGtesting.com
Printed in the USA
LVOW10s1829030717
540217LV00014B/1006/P